Snooping in the Embassy

Anna opened a door, thinking she would find a closet. It turned out to be the door to an adjoining room.

"Jessica! Come here," she cried. Jessica hurried over to her side. It was an office or study, lined with bookshelves, with a big desk in the center of the room.

"I wonder if this is where Leslie's father will be working," Jessica said.

"It seems like a secret office," said Anna.

"It would be easy to get lost in a place like this," Jessica whispered.

The two girls stepped into the room. Just then, Anna grabbed Jessica's arm. "Shhh! I heard something!"

There was a noise just outside the hall door.

"What do we do now?" Anna whispered, panic-stricken.

Then Jessica saw the door inch open. Instantly, she yanked Anna down behind an ornate Victorian screen that hid a bank of file cabinets. The girls scrunched back behind the screen as far as they could get and held their breaths. Seconds later, a man stepped into the room. . . .

IT ALL STARTED WITH

THE

SWEET VALLEY TWINS

For years teenagers across the nation have been reading about Jessica and Elizabeth Wakefield and their High School friends in SWEET VALLEY HIGH books. Now in books created especially for you, author Francine Pascal introduces you to Jessica and Elizabeth when they were 12, facing the same problems with their parents and friends that you do.

DON'T MISS ANY OF THE BOOKS IN THIS EXCITING SERIES:

SWEET VALLEY TWINS
◇ SUPER EDITION ◇

Holiday Mischief

Written by
Jamie Suzanne

Created by
FRANCINE PASCAL

BANTAM BOOKS
TORONTO • NEW YORK • LONDON • SYDNEY • AUCKLAND

SWEET VALLEY TWINS: SUPER BOOK 2: HOLIDAY MISCHIEF

A BANTAM BOOK   0 553 17633 1

First publication in Great Britain

PRINTING HISTORY
Bantam edition published 1989

Sweet Valley High and Sweet Valley Twins are
trademarks of Francine Pascal

Conceived by Francine Pascal

Bantam Books are published by Transworld Publishers Ltd.,
61–63 Uxbridge Road, Ealing, London W5 5SA,
in Australia by Transworld Publishers (Australia) Pty. Ltd.,
15–23 Helles Avenue, Moorebank, NSW 2170, and in New
Zealand by Transworld Publishers (N.Z.) Ltd., Cnr. Moselle
and Waipareira Avenues, Henderson, Auckland.

Reproduced, printed and bound in Great Britain by
Hazell Watson & Viney Limited
Member of BPCC plc
Aylesbury, Bucks, England

Holiday
Mischief

One

◇

"Lizzie! Over here!" Jessica Wakefield stood up and waved to let her identical twin know where she was sitting in the auditorium of Sweet Valley Middle School.

Elizabeth's eyes brightened at the sight of her sister and she moved quickly down the aisle toward her. "Boy, am I glad to see you!" Elizabeth cried, plopping down on the empty seat next to Jessica.

Elizabeth might as well have been looking at her mirror image. The two girls were almost impossible to tell apart. They both had blue-green eyes, the same shade of long, sun-streaked blond hair and a dimple that appeared in their left cheeks when they smiled. Only those who knew the twins well could tell them apart, until recently when they had begun to dress differently. They had even decided to wear their hair differently. Jessica usually wore hers down so the waves framed her face, while Elizabeth pinned hers back to the sides with barrettes.

When it came to interests and choice of friends, Jessica and Elizabeth were complete opposites. Of the two, Elizabeth was the quieter, more serious one. She was happy to spend time curled up with a good book or talking with her favorite friends, Amy Sutton and Julie Porter. Her biggest dream was to become a writer someday, which is why she had joined the staff of *The Sweet Valley Sixers*, the sixth grade newspaper. Jessica, unlike her twin, was happiest when she was the center of attention. She loved to gossip about who liked who, and she was a master at thinking up new schemes.

As Elizabeth settled in her seat, Jessica glanced around to see who was sitting nearby. She caught sight of Bruce Patman and flashed her most dazzling smile. Bruce was from the wealthiest family in Sweet Valley. He had brown hair and blue eyes, and Jessica and her friends agreed that he was the cutest seventh grade boy. Elizabeth thought he was the most conceited. But Jessica didn't care. She was just glad he was smiling back at her at that moment.

She nudged Elizabeth in the ribs. "Did you see that?" she whispered.

"What?" Elizabeth asked.

"Shhh! Bruce Patman is looking over here. He'll know we're talking about him," warned Jessica.

"Oh." Elizabeth shrugged. That was another difference between the twins. Recently, Jessica had become interested in boys. Ever since she had joined the Unicorn Club, an exclusive club made up of the most popular girls at school, Elizabeth claimed that all Jessica cared about was expensive clothes, cute boys and gossiping about girls who weren't even members of the club. In fact, Elizabeth often referred to the club as the "Snob Squad."

Anxious to change the subject, she asked her sister, "Do you know what they're going to talk about today?" Every Monday an all-school assembly was held in the auditorium. Most of the time the news was pretty routine, but Elizabeth had heard there was going to be a special announcement about the middle school choral group.

"Some kind of surprise, right?" Jessica turned to wave at some friends sitting in the back.

Before Elizabeth could reply, Mr. Clark, the principal, stepped up to the podium. "May I have your attention, please?" Everyone faced the stage and the students quieted down.

"Today I have the pleasure of announcing that once again, the Sweet Valley Choral Group has been selected to represent Southern California in the annual National Middle School Chorus Competition, which will be held in Washington, D.C., in early December," Mr. Clark said. Everyone clapped and cheered.

"Wow—why didn't we sign up for choir?" whispered Jessica.

"Because we had so much to do, remember?" Elizabeth reminded her twin. The girls had recently been so busy with extracurricular activities that they hadn't had a free moment in the day for another commitment. Now Elizabeth had to admit she was a little sorry that she hadn't made room in her schedule. She liked to sing, and she would have loved to see Washington!

"Because many of the other participating schools have larger choral groups, we'll need ten new members for the occasion. All students who are interested in auditioning may sign up on the sheet outside the music room. Ms. McDonald, our music teacher, and Mr. Stefan, our choral teacher, will hold auditions on Thursday right here in the auditorium."

Elizabeth and Jessica looked at each other with wide eyes. Another chance to join the choral group—*and* go to Washington! The auditorium buzzed with excited conversation.

"Remember when Ms. McDonald told us we had great soprano voices and we should be in choir?" said Jessica.

"I remember," replied Elizabeth. "And now we're going to get a second chance!"

When the assembly was dismissed, the twins

hurried to join their friends in the hall. "Can you believe it? A trip to Washington!" exclaimed Jessica, jumping up and down with her friend Ellen Riteman, who was standing with Dana Larson. Dana was already in choir and was one of the star singers.

"You won't have any trouble getting in with your voice, Jessica," Ellen said. "I just hope I get picked."

"It'll be fabulous if we can all go to Washington together!" exclaimed Jessica.

Elizabeth spotted her friends Amy Sutton and Julie Porter, and rushed to meet them. "Isn't this exciting!" she cried. "Are you trying out, Julie? You're so talented."

"Are you kidding?" Julie laughed. "I am talented, but I sure can't sing!"

"I'm going to visit my grandparents in Seattle for Christmas," said Amy. "I don't think my parents would want me to go away right before the holidays. I may not be able to go."

Another friend, Nora Mercandy, joined the group. "Are you guys trying out? I think I might. Anna Barrett said she's going to audition. Getting to go to Washington is *so* exciting."

"Jessica and I are definitely going to try out, and I'm sure the competition will be tough," said Elizabeth. "Who doesn't want to go to Washington?"

"But not everyone can sing, Lizzie," her sister said, joining her.

"Let's see if *you* can sing, Jessica," said Charlie Cashman, known as the class wise guy. He was holding up a plastic drinking cup. "Break this glass."

"Very funny, Charlie," Jessica said, but she smiled at his prank.

The bell rang, and Jessica and Elizabeth rushed off to their next class.

"We don't have a thing to worry about," said Jessica. "We've got great voices."

"But so does half the school," insisted Elizabeth. "I want to be prepared. I'm going to rehearse after school."

"Oh, Lizzie, sometimes you can be such a bore," cried Jessica, dancing ahead of her to join Lila Fowler, her best friend and a fellow Unicorn.

Elizabeth sighed. Jessica often accused her of being boring or a goody-goody. She just had to keep reminding herself that she and Jessica were very different. Jessica was impulsive, forgetful, and much too busy to worry about studying or practicing. Occasionally, Jessica even forgot to do her homework and then Elizabeth would have to come to her rescue. Still, in spite of their differences, the twins remained the best of friends.

That afternoon, the twins waited eagerly for their parents to get home so they could ask for permission to go on the trip.

Mrs. Wakefield, who worked part-time at a design firm in Sweet Valley, happened to get home first. "What fabulous news!" she exclaimed after the girls had filled her in on the trip. "Wait until your father hears about this."

Mr. Wakefield was equally enthusiastic. Both parents agreed that if the girls were chosen for the group, they would have permission to go to Washington.

"Just think, Lizzie," Jessica whispered dreamily. "We could be stars."

Elizabeth laughed. "Jess, this is a choral group, not a rock group. Nobody's going to come around and interview us for *Starstruck Magazine*."

Jessica tilted her head back so that her long hair reached down her back. "You never know," she said, winking like she had seen someone do on TV. "There are always people out there looking for new talent."

Two

◇

On Tuesday, all the students at Sweet Valley Middle School could talk about was the upcoming auditions. But all this chatter was making Elizabeth a little nervous, so she went straight home after school to rehearse. The next afternoon, Elizabeth turned down an offer to get a soda after school with her friends Amy and Julie so she could practice some more. Jessica, on the other hand, had no intention of rehearsing, and on Wednesday afternoon she went to a Unicorn Club meeting.

Finally, Thursday morning arrived. The twins stood on line with about thirty other students.

While Jessica was talking to Ellen, Elizabeth noticed that Anna Barrett, a freckle-faced, red-haired girl was standing in front of her. Elizabeth didn't know Anna very well, but she knew she was friendly with Nora Mercandy. Today she stood with her arms folded over her chest, looking very nervous and quite unhappy.

"Hi, Anna. How're you doing?" Elizabeth asked when Anna glanced her way.

Anna managed a smile. "Oh, hi, Elizabeth. Nora told me you were trying out."

"You look nervous," Elizabeth said gently. "I'm scared, too."

Anna looked around to see if anyone might be listening. Jessica was joking around with Rick Hunter, the president of the seventh grade and one of the cutest boys in school. Everyone else was busy talking, too. Anna lowered her voice. "I don't know if I should tell you this, but . . . well, you see, I can't really sing at all."

Elizabeth looked at her in amazement. "Really? Then why are you auditioning?"

"Because this is my one and only chance to get to Washington," she replied firmly.

Just then Jessica turned around and draped an arm over her sister's shoulder. "Hi, Anna. Ready for the tryout?" she asked cheerfully.

"Not really," Anna began. "I was just telling Elizabeth about my problem with singing."

"Oh, you've probably just got cold feet," said Jessica, using a term she'd heard her mother use.

"No, it's not that," Anna said. "The only reason I really want to be in the group, is because I have family in Washington."

"Oh, how great!" exclaimed Elizabeth. "I guess that means you've been to Washington before."

"Never," replied Anna. "I've never even met this part of the family before." Suddenly tears filled her eyes.

"I'm sure it'll be exciting to see them, Anna," Elizabeth said, but then she noticed that Anna was wiping away some tears. "What's wrong?"

"It's a long story. I'm not sure I should say anything," Anna said in a shaky voice.

"Anna, you can tell us," Jessica urged.

"Yes. It might help to talk about it a little," Elizabeth added.

"But my parents . . ." Anna began.

"What do they have to do with it?" Jessica asked.

Anna sighed deeply. "Well, I was adopted when I was a baby. I always knew about it. But a couple of weeks ago I found a letter to my parents about someone named Leslie, who is also adopted. Leslie is on her way to Washington from Australia—and I'm pretty sure Leslie is my real sister."

"That's wonderful! A reunion!" cried Elizabeth.

"Wait, that's not all," Anna told her. "My parents never told me anything about Leslie." She stopped and hesitated for a moment. "I wasn't meant to find out about this at all. She's thirteen . . . I always wanted an older sister. They knew that. And when I asked my parents if I could go on this Washington trip, they said it was fine with them. But they still didn't say anything about Leslie!"

"I wonder why not," Elizabeth said. "There must be a good reason why your parents are keeping this a secret, Anna."

"That's what I think, too," Anna replied, pushing her hand through her red curls. "Leslie's adoptive parents are with the Australian Consulate, and they're moving to Washington to live at the embassy. I figure it'll be easy to find Leslie with such an important father. But first I have to get into the choral group and get to Washington. That's going to be the hardest part."

"It's probably not going to be as hard as you think," Elizabeth said.

"Oh, no? Listen to this." Anna sang a few notes of "Silent Night" just to demonstrate. Her voice was scratchy and off-key.

Jessica and Elizabeth exchanged worried glances. Elizabeth knew that they were both thinking the same thing: Anna's voice was terrible. She couldn't carry a tune at all. There was no way she would ever make that group.

"Hey, Anna, I've got an idea!" cried Jessica. "Four people are auditioned at a time. Lizzie and I can stand on either side of you while we're being auditioned, and you can just mouth the words. That way it'll look like you're singing, and no one will ever have to hear you!"

"I don't know, Jess," Elizabeth said nervously. "What if someone finds out?"

"Come on, Lizzie. We have to try to help Anna," Jessica insisted. "It's perfect. What do you think, Anna?"

The line in front of them was moving quickly.

"It's almost our turn to try out," Anna said. "I don't think I have much choice. I'm willing to try if you are."

Elizabeth realized that they had to decide quickly. It didn't seem right, but she couldn't think of a better idea than Jessica's, and she wanted to help Anna.

"Okay, let's do it," Elizabeth said.

Taking a deep breath, Jessica, Elizabeth and Anna moved forward. Ellen Riteman was the fourth person in their group, and Jessica whispered a few details about the situation to her before they began.

Elizabeth was so scared for Anna that she forgot her own nervousness. Jessica and Ellen cleared their throats and coughed. Mr. Stefan looked at each singer.

"I want to hear you sing two bars of 'O, Holy Night,'" he instructed.

Elizabeth winked at Anna and then began to sing. Their voices were a little shaky at first, but then they smoothed out. Elizabeth watched out of the corner of her eye as Anna opened her mouth and pretended to sing. She could only hope that Mr. Stefan wouldn't notice that one voice was missing. But they didn't need to worry. Anna was a great actress, and she used lots of facial expressions to make it look like she was really singing.

On Friday morning when Jessica and Elizabeth got to school, kids were clustered around the main bulletin board outside the principal's office. A list of the audition winners was posted there, and every once in a while a squeal of excitement would rise from the group.

"I'm afraid to look," said Anna, covering her eyes.

"We'll look for you," offered Elizabeth. She and Jessica made their way up to the board and read down the list. Just as Anna was about to give up all hope, Jessica let out a loud whoop.

"Anna, we're in! Congratulations!" Elizabeth called to the red-headed girl.

Anna squealed and the three girls joined in an embrace.

"I'm so excited," Anna exclaimed. "I can't wait to go."

"This is wonderful. Can you believe it? December in Washington!" Elizabeth exclaimed.

"I can't wait to tell Mom and Dad we made it," said Jessica.

"I wonder what my parents will say when I tell them I'm actually going to Washington," Anna said. "Maybe then they'll tell me about Leslie."

"I'll bet they will," said Elizabeth, hoping it would be true.

"Thanks for helping me, you guys. I couldn't have gotten into the group without you."

"I'm glad we could help," Elizabeth said, smiling.

That afternoon Elizabeth and Jessica walked home from school together. "I'm eager to tell Mom and Dad our news," Elizabeth said.

"Me, too," Jessica said. "Just think, Lizzie, we really could become famous if we win. Maybe we'll even meet the President!"

"I doubt it, Jess. But it'll be exciting just to see Washington."

The twins walked in silence for a few minutes, each lost in daydreams about the upcoming trip.

Then Elizabeth said in a worried tone, "Oh, Jess, I hope we did the right thing for Anna. I feel sorry for her. I mean, I'm glad she got into the group, but now she has to pretend to be able to sing when she can't. We've got to find a way to keep Mr. Stefan from finding out the truth."

Jessica twirled and danced next to her sister. "Don't worry so much, Lizzie. We'll think of something."

The girls arrived at their house and turned up the driveway. When they walked through the kitchen door, they found their fourteen-year-old brother, Steven, standing in his favorite spot, in front of the refrigerator, pouring himself a glass of milk.

"Here come the clones—and there goes my peace and quiet!" he groaned as the twins rushed in and dropped their bookbags on the kitchen counter.

Steven was tall, with brown hair and brown eyes, and he looked very much like their father. He was a freshman at Sweet Valley High, and a member of the junior varsity basketball team. The twins couldn't understand why girls suddenly seemed so interested in him when they knew for a fact that he was a royal pain.

Jessica walked around the kitchen, sniffing.

"What's with you?" asked Steven.

"I smell food—aha!" She pointed at the half-eaten hero sandwich on the butcher block table. "I see it's feeding time at the zoo."

Elizabeth giggled. Her brother was famous for his enormous appetite.

"Very funny," growled Steven, taking his milk to the table. "If you did as much work as I do, you'd eat a lot, too."

Steven was always complaining about how hard he had to work—especially now that he was in high school.

"Poor overworked Steven," Elizabeth teased.

"Well, soon you'll only have to share the refrigerator with Mom and Dad," said Jessica.

"How come?" Steven asked with his mouth full. "Are you two moving out?"

"No, we're going to Washington, D.C.!" exclaimed Jessica.

"You're kidding," Steven replied, sounding as though he really didn't believe it.

"No, we're not kidding. We've been chosen to sing with the school choral group, which is performing in a national competition in Washington," explained Elizabeth.

For once, Steven raised his head from his sandwich and looked at them with interest. "Hey, that's great! How long will you be gone?"

"Five whole days. We're going to stay in a fancy hotel, with room service," Jessica said dreamily. "No cleaning up or dishes to do. . . ."

"Since when do you do any of those things?" challenged Steven, but his sister wasn't paying any attention to him.

Jessica kept talking. "We're going to have dinner in a different fancy restaurant every night and meet tons of exciting people."

"Give me a break," moaned Steven.

At that moment, Mr. Wakefield came marching into the kitchen. "What's this I hear about fancy hotels and restaurants?" he questioned.

Jessica proceeded to tell her father all about the trip.

"Congratulations, girls!" Mr. Wakefield exclaimed, hugging the twins. "This is a wonderful opportunity."

Mrs. Wakefield emerged from the basement and put down her laundry basket. "I could hear you all the way downstairs! What's going on in here?"

Elizabeth filled her mother in on the news.

"Oh, girls, how wonderful!" Mrs. Wakefield said.

"We have lots of hard work ahead of us," Elizabeth put in. "We have to catch up with the rest of the group."

"We won't have to, Lizzie. We're singing Christmas songs that we probably already know," Jessica explained with a wave of her hand.

"No, Jessica," Elizabeth corrected her. "I'm pretty sure the program includes some international music and some very old carols that we've never heard."

But Jessica wasn't listening. She began to waltz around the kitchen, singing. "'I'm dreaming of a white Christmas . . .'"

Steven shook his head. "Wait until you get there and find out how cold it is. Then you'll be singing a different tune."

But as the Wakefields watched Jessica, it was clear that nothing could dampen her spirits now.

Three

◇

Anna called out a greeting to her parents as she stepped in the door of their ranch-style house.

"In here!" her father yelled from the den.

Eagerly Anna ran to the den to find her mother and father hanging wallpaper. Her father was a writer and sometimes he'd write at night and work around the house during the day. Today he was wearing a pair of paint-splattered coveralls, and when he turned to look at her Anna noticed paint speckles all over his glasses and in his light brown hair.

"Hi, honey. What's up?" Mrs. Barrett asked as she smoothed a strip of wallpaper against the wall. A tall brunette woman in her thirties with light green eyes, Mrs. Barrett didn't look at all like Anna. People who didn't know Anna was adopted were always asking the Barretts where Anna got her red hair and freckles.

Anna took a deep breath and said, "Remember I asked you if I could go to Washington, D.C., with the school choral group?"

"Yes, we remember," replied Mr. Barrett.

"Well, today they announced the audition results, and I got picked!"

"Congratulations, dear!" her parents said together, hugging her in turn.

"Thanks. It's going to be so exciting. I'll be meeting lots of new people and seeing Washington for the first time ever," Anna said, hoping they would say something about Leslie.

"We're so happy for you," her mother said. "You've never been on a plane by yourself before, Anna," Mr. Barrett added. "That *is* exciting!" Then he looked at his watch. "I didn't realize it was so late. I'd better get cleaned up. We're going out to dinner. Now we even have something to celebrate. That's wonderful news, Anna."

Anna's heart sank as she watched her parents leave the room. "Wonderful news." Was that all they could say? She had almost blurted out, "Isn't there something important you want to tell me?" but she stopped herself.

Maybe there was something about her sister that they didn't want her to know. Maybe there was something about the two girls' parents that they didn't want her to know. Maybe they were afraid that Anna would want to start looking for her real parents.

"Why would they be afraid of that?" Anna asked herself aloud. Her parents had always been very open about her adoption. They had given her all the information she had ever asked for, but they had never told her about Leslie.

While her parents were upstairs getting dressed, Anna got out some old photo albums and looked for clues to the past. Maybe there would be some mention of Leslie somewhere. But she didn't find anything—just some yellowed snapshots taken of her parents when they first got married. As she sifted through the old pictures, she noticed for the thousandth time that she didn't look like her adoptive parents at all. It had bothered her when she was younger when people said there was no family resemblance. But it didn't bother her anymore.

Just as she was putting the pictures away, some papers fell out of one of the albums. Anna scooped them off the floor. Two smaller envelopes fell out of one larger one. They were old, yellowed, and faded. *Adoption papers!* Anna thought hopefully. She carefully removed the papers from the first envelope. They were definitely her adoption papers, but they gave her no clues. In the second envelope was a letter and a copy of what appeared to be someone else's adoption papers. It wasn't a very dark copy, but she was able to make out the name Leslie and the words "18 months." Then she noticed that both sets of adoption papers had the same date on them. Anna glanced at the letter that was with the papers, but all it said was:

Dear Mr. and Mrs. Barrett,
　　Perhaps these will be useful someday.
　　　　　　　　　　　　Sincerely,
　　　　　　　　　　　　M. Linwood

When Anna glanced at the outside of the envelope, she noticed that it was postmarked Australia. Here was more proof that she did indeed have a sister. Anna was newborn and her sister was eighteen months old at the time of their adoptions.

As she stared at the document, a strange feeling came over her. She felt as if she had always known about Leslie, even though she had just learned about her. It was as if a part of her had been missing all this time, a part that should be there—her sister.

Yes, that was exactly what she felt! As a little girl, Anna had had an imaginary sister, someone who was always there when she wanted her, someone to talk to in the dark. Now she wasn't so sure the sister was imaginary. She was convinced that they remembered each other in some way, and that her sister was very real.

She thought about Jessica and Elizabeth and how different they were. But they were still best friends. *Just think, there's someone in the world who probably looks a little like me,* Anna told herself. *And who probably has a lot in common with me, too.*

* * *

On Saturday morning Jessica was up first, which was unusual. But this morning was different. Jessica had to figure out what she was going to wear in Washington. She stepped over a pile of dirty laundry to get to her closet. Then she proceeded to go through and pull out her heaviest sweaters and pants, things she could wear in a colder climate. She held them up and studied herself in the full-length mirror on her closet door. She had grown a bit taller since last year and most of her clothes were too small for her now!

"What do you think?" Jessica asked the life-size poster of her favorite rock star, Johnny Buck.

Elizabeth peeked in the door. "What are you doing?" she asked. "Cleaning your closet?" She meant it as a joke—Jessica never cleaned her room unless she was forced to.

"I'm looking for some outfits to wear in Washington," Jessica cried in exasperation. "It's awful, Lizzie. I have nothing to wear! We're both going to need a whole new wardrobe!"

"I'm sure Mom is going to love that. New wardrobes for a week's visit?" Elizabeth laughed. She sat down on the bed and looked at her sister's bulging closet. Then she got up and took inventory. "I'm sure we can make do, Jess. We have warm coats."

"Make do! When we're going somewhere as glamorous as Washington! I'm asking Mom if she'll take us shopping today," Jessica decided aloud. "I want to look my best."

Elizabeth knew there was no arguing with Jessica at times like this. Jessica went downstairs to speak to their mother, and Elizabeth went back to her own room to get dressed.

At breakfast, Mrs. Wakefield said, "Why don't we go to the mall this morning. I think each of you deserves a new outfit for your trip."

Jessica squealed in delight and hugged her mother.

Once they were outside the house, Elizabeth turned to her twin. "What did you do, hypnotize her?"

Jessica grinned mischievously. "No. I just told her that we might catch cold in Washington."

The Valley Mall was crowded with Christmas shoppers.

"Everybody's got the same idea," said Mrs. Wakefield as she led the way into the girls' section of Abrams, a big department store.

Jessica found a display of purple sweaters and skirts, and set to work finding her size. Elizabeth discovered a pink and yellow sweater in a soft wool and a matching pink skirt. Mrs. Wakefield insisted on buying both girls some cold-weather boots.

She wasn't the only parent with this in mind. Jessica and Elizabeth ran into Bruce Patman and

Dana Larson in the shoe department. Dana hadn't bought anything, but Bruce was stomping around in front of a full-length mirror wearing hiking boots.

"At least we won't be the only kids from Sweet Valley wearing these," Jessica moaned as she tugged on a pair of boots.

"I know they're not high fashion, Jessica, but they'll keep you warm," said Mrs. Wakefield.

"Actually, they are in fashion," interrupted a saleswoman. She showed Jessica a picture of the same pair of boots from a popular magazine. "With these big bright-colored socks, they look super."

Jessica's eyes grew wide with excitement. "Oh, Mom, can we have the socks, too?"

Mrs. Wakefield agreed on the socks and paid for their purchases.

"I love this," Jessica breathed as they emerged from the store loaded down with packages. "I wish I lived somewhere where the seasons change all the time. Just think of all the clothes we'd have to buy!"

Four

◇

On Monday morning, Jessica and Elizabeth joined the other new choral group members for a fitting of the black robes they would wear for the competition. After school on Monday, Tuesday and Wednesday, the girls had to attend rehearsals to get them acquainted with the songs they would be singing.

At Monday's rehearsal, Mr. Stefan gave everyone an itinerary of their week in Washington and a list of rules. There would be one chaperone assigned to every six singers. There would be rehearsals every morning and an organized activity every afternoon. No one was allowed to go off on his own unless he got approval and would be with an adult. Mr. Stefan also rented a short filmstrip that showed some of the sights of the city. Everyone was so excited they could barely sit still for the film.

"Everybody's acting like this is summer vacation," Elizabeth said.

"That's how it feels, Lizzie! I can't wait to get on that plane!" cried Jessica impatiently.

After rehearsal on Tuesday, Elizabeth stopped at a bookstore and bought a guidebook and a map of Washington. When she got home, she curled up on the living room sofa with the material spread out around her.

Jessica frowned when she saw her sister. "Lizzie, why don't you just wait until you get there and be surprised?"

"Because I don't want to miss anything, Jess," Elizabeth replied. "And I don't want to waste a minute being lost."

"Nobody'll give us a chance to be lost," Jessica said. "We've got rehearsals every morning, and then guided tours and stuff in the afternoon. And chaperones the whole time—ugh!"

On Wednesday at rehearsal, Mr. Stefan stood up and announced that he wanted three singers to sing "Silent Night." "I'd like to hear Anna Barrett, Dana Larson and Jessica Wakefield please."

Anna's eyes popped wide open in surprise. Why did Mr. Stefan have to pick her? Suddenly she got chills all over and she knew she was going to be sick. "Mr. Stefan," she called, raising her hand. "I don't feel very well. May I be excused?"

"Certainly, Anna. Will you be all right?" he asked with concern.

She nodded and held her stomach, then stumbled out of the classroom to the girls' room. Some of the kids giggled.

A while later, Elizabeth realized that Anna was still in the girls' room. She raised her hand. "Mr. Stefan, may I go and see if Anna's okay? She's been gone for a while."

"Yes, Elizabeth, please do," replied Mr. Stefan.

Jessica nudged her. "Lizzie, maybe Anna doesn't want Mr. Stefan to remember that she's gone," she pointed out. "It's embarrassing having everyone know you've been hanging out in the bathroom for so long."

"That may be so, but I'm worried," said Elizabeth, getting up in the middle of "Silent Night."

She went out of the room and met Anna heading back toward the rehearsal room. "I really was sick, Elizabeth," Anna said, looking pale.

"Oh, no," Elizabeth said. "That's too bad." Then she got an idea. "But being sick might get you out of rehearsal today and then Mr. Stefan won't hear you sing."

When they returned to their seats, Mr. Stefan asked Anna how she was feeling.

"Much better, thank you," she replied.

Then he said, "Anna, even if you're feeling better, I don't want you to strain your voice today.

We want to save our voices for the competition. It's not worth it to push yourself in rehearsal and then have no voice left for the real event."

Anna looked at Elizabeth and Jessica, then sighed with relief. Jessica giggled. "Wow, Anna, you'd better not say anything. You might strain your voice."

Some of the boys began making odd-sounding loud noises to demonstrate how they, too, could strain their voices.

"All right, class, let's get on with our rehearsal," called Mr. Stefan in a firm tone.

On Thursday morning, the twins were up early to do some last-minute packing. Mrs. Wakefield checked their suitcases to make sure they had everything they needed before Mr. Wakefield loaded the van.

"Jessica, put your hat and gloves into your carry-on bag," Mrs. Wakefield said. "It will probably be cold when you get off the plane."

Jessica smiled brightly. "Oh, Mom, I won't need it," she said, but she did as she was told.

"Jessica's going to bring the California weather with her to Washington," Steven joked.

The entire Wakefield family went to the airport to see the twins off. When it was time to board the plane, Jessica turned to her parents with unexpected tears in her eyes.

"Oh, I'm going to miss you both so much!" she cried, hugging them tightly.

"You'll only be away for five days, Jessica, not a whole year," Mrs. Wakefield reminded her daughter.

"And remember all those fancy people and those parties?" Mr. Wakefield said.

Elizabeth giggled. "Yes, and snow, Jess. Don't forget about the snow."

"And the food, Jess," Steven told his sister. "Have lobster for me, will you?"

Jessica let go of her parents and ran over to hug her brother. Steven hugged her back.

"Quick, take a picture," Elizabeth told her father. "Or no one will ever believe that this happened."

Everyone laughed and Steven turned red. "I was just trying to be nice."

Elizabeth hugged her family and then said goodbye. As she and Jessica headed through the gate and onto the plane, Elizabeth spotted Anna with her parents and waved.

"Remember to call us as soon as you get there," Mrs. Barrett told her daughter.

"I will, Mom," replied Anna. Some students were milling around. Some were already lined up and ready to board the plane.

"I'm sorry we can't be there to hear you sing," said Anna's father.

Actually, Anna figured he would probably be sorry if he could hear her sing, but she didn't say so. Instead, she thought about Leslie. She was so disappointed that neither of her parents had said a word about her sister!

She kissed them goodbye and boarded the plane. As she took one last backward glance, she felt as though her parents were strangers. How could they keep such a secret from her? Didn't they want her to be happy? She tried to tell herself they had a good reason for doing this, but it still hurt.

Inside, Elizabeth and Jessica were seated side by side toward the front of the plane. Luckily, the plane was not too full.

"Anna! Sit with us!" Elizabeth called.

"Hi, Jessica. Hi, Elizabeth. Thanks, I was hoping I would get to sit with you," Anna said gratefully.

"How're you doing?" Jessica asked as Anna sat down next to her.

"I'm excited about the trip, but I'm still disappointed that my parents didn't say a word about Leslie. I was sure when they heard I was going to Washington they would tell me all about her."

"Maybe they haven't put two and two together," suggested Jessica.

"With any luck, you'll get to meet Leslie while we're in Washington, and then you can talk to your parents about it when you get back," Elizabeth said sympathetically.

"I hope so," replied Anna.

As soon as the plane took off, everyone started talking at once. They were interrupted by Ms. MacDonald.

"Boys and girls! As you know, we are not alone in this plane, so please keep your excited chatter down to a low roar."

"Does anyone want to play Crazy Eights?" suggested Elizabeth.

"Yes!" answered Anna, Jessica and Ellen in unison.

When they had finished playing, Elizabeth sat back and read from her guidebook. "We can go into the Lincoln Memorial, and we can see the National Gallery of Art and the Smithsonian Institution," she suggested.

"I just want to go through the Capitol Building," said Bruce Patman.

"I want to see the cherry blossoms," added Anna.

"They don't have cherry blossoms at this time of year," Elizabeth said, laughing. "It's all snow." Then she read aloud about the cherry blossoms. "They arrived from Japan as a gift, but they were all infected with diseases and insects. The Japanese had to send another shipment of trees."

"Just what we all wanted to know, Lizzie," Jessica commented. "Just think of all the things we're going to see while we're there; snow, celebrities. Maybe we'll even get to go ice skating," she went on dreamily.

"I want to go to the Library of Congress," Elizabeth told everyone. "And to the National Archives to see the Constitution."

"Hey, that sounds great!" exclaimed Ellen. "I'd like to see what the Constitution really looks like."

"Oh, it's probably just a photocopy," joked Bruce Patman. Everyone laughed.

"A tour of the White House has already been arranged for us," Elizabeth told the others.

"Anything else, Ms. Know-It-All?" Jessica teased. Elizabeth made a face at her twin, and everyone laughed.

It was dark when the plane landed in Washington. Once everyone had collected their luggage, they walked outside to a waiting bus. The air was crisp and cold, and Elizabeth buttoned up her coat as she stepped out of the terminal and into the bus.

"Where's the snow?" cried Jessica.

"It's supposed to snow tonight, young lady," the bus driver told her. "Just for you."

Elizabeth thought Washington looked like a giant twinkling star. She looked out the window as the bus traveled alongside the Potomac River.

She consulted her guidebook to identify the Pentagon and Arlington Cemetery beyond it. As soon as the bus crossed the Potomac, she spotted the Lincoln Memorial.

The bus driver was also kind enough to point

out the sights to the group. "From the Lincoln Memorial, we go through Constitution Gardens. The Washington Monument on your right. And these are federal buildings."

"There's the White House!" somebody yelled from the back of the bus. Everyone turned to look out the windows.

"Now I feel like I'm really in Washington," Elizabeth said.

"Me, too. Isn't it glamorous?" Jessica cried, pressing her nose to the cold window. "Look! The Christmas tree on the White House lawn! Just what I wanted to see!"

About five minutes later, the bus drew up outside the Whitney Hotel, an old-fashioned, elegant building with doormen outside and a red carpet on the sidewalk.

Mrs. Isaacs, a thin, energetic woman with short gray hair, had been assigned chaperone for Jessica, Elizabeth, Ellen, Anna and two other girls. She helped them out of the bus with their luggage and directed them into the hotel lobby.

Jessica set down her bags and looked around the luxurious lobby. The dark red carpeting and heavy, gold-trimmed drapes looked very rich against the gold-and-glass chandeliers. There were glass-topped tables and antique brocade couches and chairs against the walls. Beautifully dressed men and women were sitting and talking or making their way toward the elevators.

"This place looks like something on TV," Jessica whispered in awe. "The people are so perfect they don't seem real."

At that moment, a porter whisked away her luggage and put it on a trolley to take upstairs.

She sighed. "I could get used to this," she said. "Dressing up every day and being waited on constantly. I want to stay here forever!"

"Jess, what're you saying?" cried Elizabeth, feeling a little hurt. "You love Sweet Valley!"

"Yes, well, I do," Jessica responded. "But it isn't very elegant. It's just an ordinary town."

Sweet Valley was a beautiful oceanside suburb with nearly perfect weather. Both Elizabeth and Jessica thought it was the greatest place to live. Or, at least, they always had. Elizabeth couldn't believe how quickly Jessica could change her mind.

"We just got here, Jess," Elizabeth reminded her. "You don't really know if you're going to like it or not."

"Yes, I do," Jessica insisted.

Before either of them could say another word, they noticed a very pretty, brown-haired girl, about their age, standing nearby. She was wearing a silky red dress with sequins sewn around the neckline. Her confident smile made her look like someone very important.

"I wonder if she's from one of the competing schools," Jessica said to her sister.

"Probably," Elizabeth replied. "There are at

least two other schools that are staying at this hotel. Grant Middle School from Columbus, Ohio, and Brent Middle School from Atlanta, Georgia."

"Dana Larson told me that Grant has won the competition for the past three years," exclaimed Ellen. "She's heard they're fantastic."

"Uh, oh," Jessica said. "Sounds like tough competition."

Mrs. Isaacs came over to them. "Come, girls. It's time to go upstairs and get to bed. We've had an exhausting day, and you must all rest so that your voices are good and strong tomorrow."

Elizabeth looked back across the lobby at the brown-haired girl. She had joined a friend and was walking away from them. Then she glanced at Jessica. Sometimes Elizabeth could look at her sister and know what she was thinking. This was one of those times, and they were both thinking, "It's going to be a tough competition!"

Five

"Jessica! We have to be downstairs in five minutes!" cried Elizabeth, shaking her sister urgently. It was Friday morning, their first full day in Washington.

Jessica felt her sister's hand on her shoulder, but she didn't feel like moving. She pulled the covers over her ears and tried to ignore Elizabeth. She wanted to go on sleeping—and dreaming.

"We've got to get to rehearsal, Jess! Come on. It's snowing!" Elizabeth added as a last resort.

At the mention of snow, Jessica began to stir. "It's snowing?" she repeated groggily, pulling back the covers and hopping out of bed.

"Whew! I thought you'd never get up!" Elizabeth exclaimed, yanking back the heavy drapes. "Look outside. Isn't it beautiful?"

Jessica gazed out at the silent flakes drifting through the air. Then she looked at the white landscape.

"Wow, I can't wait to go outside," she said. Suddenly she had forgotten how tired she was from the long plane flight. She put on a pair of wool pants and a heavy green sweater.

Elizabeth was already dressed and ready to go.

Mrs. Isaacs bustled into the room just as Jessica was applying some mascara.

"Remember your hats, girls. It's cold out there," she warned. Dutifully, Elizabeth put on her white wool hat, but Jessica refused. "It'll mess up my hair," she explained.

"You'll also catch pneumonia," Mrs. Isaacs warned as they hurried out the door. Ellen and Anna emerged from their room to join them in the hallway.

"Hi, everyone," called Anna a little nervously. "Did you see the snow?"

"Yes!" Jessica and Elizabeth chorused.

Jessica took one look at Anna and stopped short. "Excuse me. I left something in my room," she told Mrs. Isaacs.

"Go ahead, but hurry up," Mrs. Isaacs called.

Jessica joined the group just in time to hop on the bus to the auditorium. Everyone was moaning about not having time to eat breakfast.

"Just think," Jessica said brightly. "We'll be able to eat twice as much at lunch."

During the ride, Elizabeth pointed out some sights.

"There's Dupont Circle, the National Zoological Park, and Woodley Park Zoo," she said.

"Our tour guide," teased Jessica. "She's been reading up on it for days."

"Where can we go sledding?" asked Winston Egbert.

"Sorry, Winston, it doesn't say," said Elizabeth.

When they got to the auditorium, the students scrambled off the bus and started making snowballs.

Charlie Cashman threw one at Jessica and Anna, and hit Jessica right in the back.

Just as they were entering the building, someone hit Anna with a snowball and she and Jessica turned to see who it was. The pretty brown-haired girl they'd seen the day before was standing with a group of friends, laughing and pointing at Anna.

"I'll bet it was her," Jessica suggested.

"Oh, Jessica, I found out who she is," Ellen told her. "She's Sherrie Dunston, Grant's superstar soprano!"

Jessica's spirits fell. By looks alone, she knew the girl was her biggest competition. And now she found out she had a great voice, too. Sherrie Dunston would be hard to beat.

"Come on, Jess. We're going to get lost!" Elizabeth cried, pulling Jessica along by the hand.

The auditorium was next to a small recital hall. The auditorium itself had a huge stage. Heavy purple velvet curtains were draped across the front of the stage. Overhead, old-fashioned chandeliers hung from a carved ceiling. Jessica was impressed. She had never seen anything so majestic in Sweet Valley.

Each school was to rehearse separately and take turns using the stage. Sweet Valley was scheduled to be first this morning.

Mr. Stefan motioned the girls toward the stage. "All right, class. Everyone in a straight line. We are going to choose our soloists this morning. By now, you've all had a chance to look over your music and are quite familiar with the repertoire. I'd like to have each of you sing a few lines solo for me."

"Solos! I can't do a solo!" Anna whispered hoarsely.

"Shhh. Don't worry," Jessica muttered under her breath. "Leave it to me."

"Now, let's begin," said Mr. Stefan, raising his conducting stick. A hush fell over the room.

Jessica pretended to fumble with a pen in the front pocket of her sweater. Then, while no one was looking, she squirted something at Anna. A dark, wet spot spread across Anna's white sweater.

Anna gasped. The sound echoed in the quiet auditorium. Ellen and Elizabeth turned and looked at Anna in horror. Across the auditorium, Sherrie Dunston turned and stared at Anna, too.

"Oh, no! Your beautiful sweater!" cried Elizabeth, blotting at the spots with a tissue.

"Oh, I'm so sorry! My pen leaked," wailed Jessica, holding her pen at arm's length.

"I'll never get these horrible stains out," Anna moaned.

Elizabeth ran to the rest room and came back with wet paper towels. As she dabbed at the ink, it spread into an even bigger blotch.

Anna was sorry about the sweater. It was her favorite and it was new. But she was also a little relieved. She winked at Jessica. This was her opportunity to get out of the solo! She turned to Mr. Stefan. "May I be excused so I can change, Mr. Stefan?"

Mr. Stefan frowned at the mess on Anna's sweater. "Yes, Anna, of course."

"Hey, Jessica!" cried Bruce. "How about getting ink all over me?"

Everyone started talking and laughing at once. Mr. Stefan turned his attention to the students. "OK now, class. It's just a little ink—nothing to get so excited about. Quiet down and let's get started with our solos."

"If it's OK I'll go back to the hotel with Anna, Mr. Stefan," Elizabeth offered.

The teacher notified Mrs. Isaacs to expect the two girls and Anna and Elizabeth took a cab back to the hotel.

* * *

On the way out, Elizabeth noticed Sherrie Dunston staring at them. *I wonder what she thinks of this?* Elizabeth thought as she and Anna climbed into the cab.

"Jessica ruined my sweater, but she saved my life, too," Anna said as they sat back in the seats.

"What a way to do it," Elizabeth replied. "But at least it worked."

"No kidding. Can you imagine me singing a solo, Elizabeth?" Anna asked. "I guess it was the best thing that could've happened."

Elizabeth had to agree that she couldn't imagine Anna singing a solo. She sighed. "I guess so, but I still feel awful about your sweater. . . ."

"Look! The ink has disappeared!" exclaimed Anna, looking down at her sweater.

Sure enough, the huge spot had faded completely. Elizabeth couldn't believe it. "It's magic!" she breathed.

"Wow, it must be disappearing ink," Anna exclaimed. "What a genius she is!"

Elizabeth had to admit that Jessica's idea really was pretty fantastic.

At the hotel, Mrs. Isaacs examined Anna's white sweater. "Why, there's no ink on this at all!" she exclaimed. "How did you get it off?"

"It was easy," said Anna, winking at Elizabeth.

"Maybe it wasn't the kind of ink that stains," Elizabeth suggested.

"Maybe," said Mrs. Isaacs, but she looked doubtful. "Anyway, you should both go back to the rehearsal. I'll call another cab."

Anna changed into a different sweater. Then the two girls traveled back to the auditorium.

When they arrived, Jessica was ecstatic. She bounced over to her sister and Anna. "Guess what! I got the very best part in the performance! I'm singing the lead solo part in 'The Little Drummer Boy.' That's the biggest and most important piece in the whole program!"

"That's fantastic, Jess," Elizabeth said. She was always pleased when something wonderful happened to her sister. She was equally pleased that Jess's plan had saved Anna from total embarrassment.

There was still some time left for rehearsal when Anna and Elizabeth got back to the auditorium. Mr. Stefan asked Elizabeth to sing a verse of "What Child Is This?"

"Very good!" he exclaimed. "That was the last solo part and I'll be assigning it to you, Elizabeth."

"Congratulations, Elizabeth!" Anna cried. "I'm so glad you didn't miss out because of me."

Elizabeth smiled. She was glad, too.

As they were leaving the rehearsal hall, they heard one of the other groups practicing in a nearby room. A single, clear soprano voice wafted out into the auditorium.

"Who's that?" Bruce Patman asked.

"Sherrie Dunston," answered Dana knowingly. "I'd know that voice anywhere. She's from Grant, the school that will be our strongest competition."

"I guess we've got a lot of work to do to get that good," Winston added.

"We can beat them," Dana said with determination and everyone cheered.

As they were leaving the building, Sherrie Dunston passed Anna and said loud enough for everyone to hear, "If your voice is anything like your manners, you're in real trouble."

Sherrie's friends giggled. Anna's cheeks burned. "Just what is that supposed to mean?" she cried, glaring at Sherrie.

Sherrie shrugged and smiled. "Just what I said. Anyone messy enough to get ink all over her sweater has to be a lousy singer."

"That's really nasty," Elizabeth told her hotly. "It wasn't Anna's fault."

Sherrie ignored the comment. Jessica rushed into the conversation. "What has Anna ever done to you, Miss Priss?" she demanded, and then she imitated Sherrie's manner.

"Do you always butt in where you're not wanted?" Sherrie demanded. "Who asked you anyway?"

Jessica put her hands on her hips. "Nobody has to ask me. You don't have any right to talk to our friend Anna like that."

"I can do anything I want," Sherrie shot back.

Angrily, she tossed her long dark hair over her shoulders and flounced away from them.

"I wonder why she picked on you, Anna," Jessica said.

"Well, with ink spurting all over me, I guess I stood out," Anna suggested. "And it's a good way to throw your competition off balance."

Elizabeth thought that maybe Jessica's plan had backfired a little. The kind of attention she had drawn to Anna hadn't been exactly positive. What would Sherrie do next? Elizabeth looked over at her twin. Obviously, Jessica was thinking the same thing.

"I'll bet we haven't seen the last of Sherrie Dunston," Jessica said as they all watched the pretty girl disappear onto the Grant bus.

Six

◇

On Friday afternoon, the Sweet Valley Choral Group took a bus tour of Washington, including a visit to the White House and the Smithsonian. Elizabeth brought along her guidebook, although the tour guide, Mr. Scope, was able to fill them in on just about everything.

"This is an exciting city," Mr. Scope announced into a microphone. "There are a lot of powerful people here and big decisions are made almost every day." They passed a man standing on a street corner handing out pamphlets. "See? Everybody wants to be president in this town."

Laughter echoed through the bus and then Mr. Scope continued. "Going down Sixteenth Street toward the White House, you've got embassies on your right and left. There are a hundred and thirty-one foreign embassies in the District of Columbia."

The wide, tree-lined boulevard was bordered by sleek modern buildings as well as ornate, old ones.

"Which one is the Australian Embassy?" Anna asked, pressing her nose to the cold glass.

"That one." Mr. Scope pointed to a sleek glass building bordered by trees. "Do you see the blue flag with the stars and the small English flag in the corner?"

As they passed by the girls memorized the location for future reference. Elizabeth had a feeling they would be spending some time at the Australian Embassy, although she didn't know exactly how it was going to happen. No one was allowed to leave the hotel without a chaperone's permission.

At the end of Sixteenth Street was the White House, surrounded by snow-covered lawns. Seeing the impressive building in daylight was really exciting.

Jessica and Elizabeth got off the bus and made their way up to the White House entrance. They sailed through the whole tour gasping and exclaiming over everything.

"The Blue Room—isn't that the most fabulous room you ever saw?" Jessica cried.

She was still talking about it when they got back to the bus. The tour continued to the Washington Monument, the white-columned Jefferson Memorial, and finally the U.S. Capitol. Here, everyone was allowed to get out and take pictures. Jessica kept looking around, hoping to catch a glimpse of somebody famous. "Just think what Lila would say if we got a picture of the president," she said to Ellen.

Ellen laughed. "She would probably like it better if you got a picture of Johnny Buck."

Jessica laughed and then reboarded the bus. The next stop was the Smithsonian Institution, which was full of trains, musical instruments, apothecary jars, clocks and weathercocks. There was even an exhibit featuring Christopher Columbus's books on navigation and his letters to King Ferdinand and Queen Isabella. The museum guide was especially helpful in answering all of the students' questions.

"I don't know about anyone else, but I'm dying to go sledding," Jerry McAllister said when they came to the end of their tour.

A cheer rose from the group.

"All right, everyone. Mr. Scope tells me there is a local park where you can go sledding and a rental shop nearby where we can get the sleds. Anyone who wants to participate can meet me in the hotel lobby in 15 minutes," Mrs. Isaacs shouted above the noise of the students.

Within five minutes of arriving at their hotel, the entire Sweet Valley Choral Group was back in the lobby, bundled up for the snow. "I'll bet nobody gets ready for school this quickly," joked Jessica.

When they arrived at the park, the whole group burst from the bus and ran across the snow, laughing and throwing snowballs. Jessica and Elizabeth watched a small group break away and start building a snowman.

The girls trudged up the slope that many kids were sledding down. Anna placed her sled down, braced her feet against the steering bar and took off down the hill. "Wow!" cried Elizabeth. "She looks like she really knows what she's doing!"

When Anna got back to the top of the hill, Elizabeth and Jessica asked her to teach them what she knew.

"How'd you learn this?" Jessica asked.

"My parents take me to the Sierras every year," Anna explained. "We go sledding and skiing. I love it."

Jessica and Elizabeth decided to go down the hill together on one sled the first time. Elizabeth clung tightly to Jessica's waist while Jessica steered wildly down the steep incline. Both of them loved the thrill of racing down the hill.

"Let's do it again, Lizzie," Jessica begged, scrambling to her feet.

As they approached the top of the slope, Elizabeth noticed Sherrie Dunston and a group of her schoolmates gathered nearby with their sleds in hand.

"I guess this is a popular place," said Anna.

Sherrie Dunston strolled toward Jessica. "Fancy meeting you here," she said sweetly. "Why don't we have a sledding race? Grant against Sweet Valley?" she suggested loudly.

"All right!" both teams cried in unison.

"At least we agree on something," Jessica said.

Elizabeth was nervous. She motioned for the other Sweet Valley students to gather around so they could talk privately. "Look, we're from California and these kids are from Ohio. We don't know the first thing about snow or sledding."

Jessica sighed. "Yeah, that's true. But we can learn, Lizzie. It didn't seem all that hard just now. All you have to do is steer, the snow does the rest. And besides, we've got Anna on our team. She's pretty good!"

Bruce Patman and Colin Harmon joined the group. "Hey, I've been skiing before, Elizabeth," Bruce offered. "I know I can handle a sled."

"Yeah, me, too," said Colin. I know how to skateboard. It's not so different."

"This isn't a sidewalk, Colin," Elizabeth said, looking down the snowy hill. "But we might as well try it," she said giving in.

Sherrie was marching around, talking to her teammates.

"Let's all line up in relay-type lines, one against one," Sherrie shouted so everyone could hear.

Jessica dragged her sled to the end of the quickly-forming line at the same time as Sherrie. They glared at each other, and Jessica's mittened fingers tightened into fists.

Dana Larson had taken charge of being the starter. When she saw Jessica, she whispered, "Good luck against Sherrie, and watch out. She'll do anything to win."

Before Jessica could reply, Dana turned toward the starting line and yelled: "Ready, set, go-o-o!" Two sleds shot down the slope.

Jessica looked over to see who the two beginning sledders were, but she couldn't tell. Next in line was Anna.

"There goes the team slob," said Sherrie.

Jessica ignored her remark. "Go, Anna!" she screamed, and her voice was joined by those of her teammates. Anna pushed off and hurtled down the snowy mountain, her hair streaming out behind her like a red banner.

"I guess it's you against me," Sherrie said softly, smiling a deadly smile.

"Then I guess you'd better watch out," countered Jessica. She didn't want Sherrie to think for a moment that she was afraid. Or that any of the Sweet Valley kids weren't as good as the Grant kids.

Sherrie laughed. "Growing up in Ohio has its advantages," she said.

"Well, we have the Sierras," Jessica reminded her. "And they have much better snow."

Jessica had no idea what she was talking about, but she thought it sounded good.

"The amount of the snow doesn't matter," Sherrie replied, grinning. "You can sled on rocks if you're good."

Jessica swallowed hard. She didn't want Sherrie to guess, but her heart was pounding. For once, Jessica wished it was Anna against Sherrie. Now she saw Anna trudging up the slope, looking triumphant. Ahead of Jessica, Elizabeth sat on her sled, next to a Grant girl named Tara Devlin.

As Elizabeth shoved off, Jessica screamed, "Go, Lizzie!" Elizabeth tore off down the mountain, her white hat bobbing as she flew over the bumps. She seemed to be headed straight down, and then all of a sudden, her sled tipped slightly and she was off, thudding onto the snow. Anna went to help her up.

"Looks like your team is dropping like flies," Sherrie said, grinning at Jessica.

Jessica glared at her opponent. "We'll see about that."

Winston took over the starter job for Dana so that she could take her turn. Pitted against a Grant boy, Dana flew down the hill with ease, but she lost her balance about halfway down and ran into a snowbank.

At last it was Jessica and Sherrie's turn.

"Come on, Jessica!" cried Colin Harmon.

Jessica smiled at her friends and her twin and gave them the thumbs up sign.

Sherrie pulled her sled up to the starting line. Jessica brought hers up right next to Sherrie, but not too close. The girls hunched forward, ready to fly. Jessica was angry and Sherrie was just waiting for her to make a mistake. Well, Jessica Wakefield would show her!

"Ready . . . set . . . go!" screamed Dana. Jessica shoved herself forward. Snow flew up and stung her face, but it felt good. The sled sliced nicely through the snow, sliding straight down the hill. Jessica thought she was doing pretty well. She looked around and saw Sherrie behind her, headed straight for her.

What's she doing? Jessica wondered. The idea was to go straight down the hill, and see who could get to the finish line first. She had the uneasy feeling that Sherrie was up to something.

Behind her, Sherrie dodged first to the left, then to the right. Jessica was totally confused, and she felt her sled losing speed. Then, realizing that that was exactly what Sherrie wanted to happen, she steered her sled over a steep part so that it would go faster. Almost instantly, Sherrie appeared next to her.

Jessica caught Sherrie's nasty smile in the split second before the brown-haired girl drove her sled directly across Jessica's path. Jessica screamed and yanked on her rope to try to steer her sled out of the way, but it swerved violently. When she looked up, she was headed straight for a tree!

Frantically, Jessica tried to steer the sled, but

there wasn't time. With a loud crash, the sled hit the tree, throwing her off, face-first into the snow. Somewhere in the distance, she heard shouts and laughter.

Jessica raised her face and brushed the snow out of her hair with the back of her hand.

"Are you OK?" someone asked.

She looked up and met a pair of dark green eyes. They belonged to a cute boy from the Grant team who had run down the hill to see if she was hurt. Jessica was speechless for a moment.

"Uh, yes, I think so," she mumbled, brushing snow from her jacket. He took her arm and helped her up.

"No broken bones? You really hit that tree hard," he said, smiling warmly at her.

"No, I think I'm all right, thanks," replied Jessica. "I'm Jessica Wakefield, by the way."

"Yeah, I know. I'm Matt Halpin, one of your enemies," he said, grinning.

"You're sure the nicest enemy I ever had," Jessica told him. Laughing, they walked back up the hill, dragging the sled behind them.

"Want to know a secret?" he said in a low voice. Jessica nodded. "Sherrie Dunston may be the best singer we've got, but she's a horrible person. Sometimes she can be really nasty."

"So I've noticed," Jessica said, but she didn't want to waste time talking about Sherrie.

"The trouble is, nobody on our team dares to tell her off," Matt continued.

Jessica was pleased that Matt had confided in her about Sherrie. Secretly, she wanted to be the one to tell Sherrie Dunston off.

When Matt and Jessica got to the top of the hill, Sherrie was already there. She glared at Jessica.

Everyone on both teams stopped talking and stared at Jessica and Matt. Elizabeth rushed over to her sister. "Jess, are you okay? Sherrie is furious that she didn't win that run because of the mean trick she played on you."

"Serves her right," added Anna.

Jessica nodded, then looked at Matt. "Oh, uh, this is Matt Halpin. He's the nicest enemy we have."

The girls laughed.

Jessica marched over to Sherrie. "How about a rematch?" Sherrie grinned. "Sure. Why not? This should be easy."

"Let's see if she can go straight this time," Jessica whispered to Elizabeth. Sherrie drew her sled up next to Jessica's. Dana shouted, "Go!" and the two sleds shot down the hill, spraying snow out behind them.

Sherrie was zooming along ahead of Jessica when Jessica suddenly moved up next to her and smiled. When she got to the bottom first, she jumped off her sled and turned around to wave to her friends. "I won, I won," she shouted, as Sherrie glided past her, scowling.

Jessica laughed. "Hey, Sherrie, aren't you going to congratulate me?"

But Sherrie didn't say a word. She just stood up, grabbed her sled, and stomped up the hill.

When they returned to the hotel, Jessica noticed a novelty shop just a few doors from the entrance. She looked at the various items in the window, hoping to get an idea for the perfect revenge on Sherrie.

Upstairs in the twins' hotel room, Anna was looking up the Australian Embassy's telephone number while the others were getting ready for dinner. "May I have the direct number for Mr. Linwood, please?" she asked when she got through to the embassy.

"At Mr. Linwood's request, we can't give out that information," said the operator.

Anna's spirits sank. She hung up the phone and said, "Then the only way is to sneak out to the embassy myself. But how am I going to pull that off?"

Jessica stood in the doorway dressed in her new purple outfit. "Shhh! You don't want Mrs. Isaacs to hear, do you?" she whispered. "We'll talk about it at dinner. Come on, let's go downstairs."

Jessica, Elizabeth, and Anna discussed the problem during dinner in the big dining room behind the lobby. "Look, Anna, maybe we can sneak out tonight, after everyone is asleep," Jessica suggested, taking a huge spoonful of chocolate mousse.

"I don't think that's a good idea, Jess," Elizabeth told her sister. "For one thing, Mrs. Isaacs is in the room with us, and second, we'd have to get past all the doormen downstairs. And third, if we got caught, we'd get kicked out of the competition!"

"You'd have to do something really bad to get kicked out of the competition," someone interrupted.

Elizabeth looked up and saw Sherrie Dunston standing beside their table. The color drained from Anna's cheeks as Sherrie turned her gaze to her. She wondered how much of their conversation Sherrie had heard.

"In fact," Sherrie went on, staring straight at Anna, "I know that they kick you out if you can't sing."

Anna felt faint. Did Sherrie know her terrible secret? It wouldn't be that hard to figure out, now that she thought about it.

"Who asked you?" demanded Jessica hotly.

"I'll just bet you can't even sing a note, Anna," Sherrie continued. "And that is definitely against the rules!"

"That's not true!" Anna cried, jumping up from her seat. Her voice cracked in midsentence and she felt like crying.

Sherrie let out a tinkly little laugh. *Even her laughter is musical*, Anna thought with despair. In comparison, Anna sounded like a frog under the best of circumstances.

Jessica stood up and moved very close to Sherrie, close enough that Sherrie started to back away. "Anna wouldn't be in this group if she couldn't sing. You're just afraid that we're better than you. And you're right to be scared because we *are* better than you."

Sherrie laughed again, and Anna could tell from her smile that she knew Jessica was only bluffing.

Seven

◇

On Saturday morning, Anna got up earlier than the others and quickly threw on some clothes. Snow was falling outside for the second day in a row.

When she walked outside the hotel, there were a few other Sweet Valley students playing in the snow before rehearsal. One group had already built a small snowman. Dana Larson was wrapping her own scarf around the snowman's neck when Anna approached her.

"Here are a couple of stones for eyes," Anna offered.

"Oh, thanks. Doesn't he look cute?" Dana asked, laughing. "I've never made a snowman before."

"If there was more snow, we could lie down in it and make angels by waving our arms and legs," Anna said.

Just then Sherrie came out dressed in a gorgeous purple-and-lavender snowsuit. Snowflakes stuck prettily in her dark hair and on her eyelashes. She made a beeline for Anna.

"Hi. How's your voice today? I'll bet you can't sing 'God Bless America,'" Sherrie said to Anna. "In fact, I'll bet you can't sing at all."

Anna was determined not to get upset. "Of course I can," she replied. Of course, she wouldn't dare sing in front of Sherrie.

"Do it, then," Sherrie insisted, resting her hands on her hips.

"I'm saving my voice for rehearsal," Anna replied nervously. Everyone gathered around the two girls.

"Yeah, leave her alone," Dana chimed in.

"Why don't you sing, Anna?" Bruce Patman asked. "Show her you can."

Anna was petrified. The others didn't know she couldn't sing, and she knew they wanted her to prove Sherrie wrong. Nobody had any trouble singing that song—especially not a member of the Sweet Valley Choral Group! Nobody, that is, except Anna Barrett.

Colin Harmon nudged Anna. "What's wrong? Why don't you just sing it so she'll stop being a pain."

"It's the principle," Anna replied. "She's just bullying me, and I won't give in."

"That's right, Anna," Dana agreed. "Good for you."

"Anna, it's no big deal. It's just a song. You can't even sing a simple song?" Sherrie asked.

"No, I just won't. I won't, I won't!" cried Anna.

Elizabeth was just entering the lobby at that moment and she quickly ran outside to see what was happening. Sherrie was standing in the middle of a crowd of kids, arms folded, looking smug and superior. Anna was shouting at Sherrie, but Elizabeth could see she was close to tears.

Elizabeth raced over to Anna and said, "Anna, your voice! You remember what the doctor and Mr. Stefan said! You're going to get too sick to sing if you don't listen to them!" she exclaimed. "And even worse, what are you doing out here in the cold?"

"She's not sick! She never said she was sick!" Sherrie insisted angrily. "Anyone can see she's fine. She just can't sing, that's all. This proves it."

"It doesn't prove *anything*!" Anna cried hotly.

"Sherrie, why don't you go stick your head in the snow and cool off?" Dana challenged.

Elizabeth and Anna started for the door. "Just leave our team alone, Sherrie. Mind your own business," Elizabeth told her.

Once they were alone in the elevator, Elizabeth said, "I don't know why she's picking on you, Anna. But I think you'd better come down with laryngitis—right away. Nobody can sing with laryngitis."

"That's for sure. But then they won't let me outside, either," wailed Anna.

"Well, that's a chance you'll have to take," replied Elizabeth. "You don't have much of a choice, you know."

Elizabeth opened the door to the suite to find Jessica pacing back and forth across the room. "Where have you been? Ellen and I were beginning to worry," she exclaimed. "We were just about to go downstairs and look for you," said Ellen, who was sitting on a chair pulling on her boots.

"You wouldn't have had to look too far," Anna said. She went on to explain what had happened. As she talked, Jessica got more and more angry. "Someone has to stop her. She's really after Anna—and me. There's got to be some way to get back at her."

"Jess, don't do anything silly," Elizabeth warned. "You don't want to get kicked out of the competition." Elizabeth knew her twin had a way of getting into trouble rather easily.

Jessica rolled her eyes. "Don't worry so much, Lizzie. I won't do anything crazy. I'll just play a small trick on Sherrie."

"Look, promise me one thing," Elizabeth said. "Whatever you do, be careful. And let's agree on something else—from now on Anna has laryngitis, OK? Just so we have our stories straight."

"Sure," Jessica replied absently. Ellen and Anna agreed.

Elizabeth sighed. Once Jessica made up her mind to do something, there was no stopping her.

In between rehearsal and lunch, Jessica and Ellen sneaked out of their rooms and went downstairs to the novelty shop.

As the girls peered through the glass case at the merchandise, a saleswoman asked if she could help them.

"Yes. I want something really creepy and scary," Jessica said. "I want to play a practical joke on someone."

"Hmmm. Let's see . . . " the saleswoman said. "We have some battery-operated hands over here." She took one out and showed them how the fingers wiggled.

Jessica and Ellen liked the hand, but it was too big for what they had in mind.

"Thanks," Jessica said. "But I think we'll look around some more."

Finally, after walking up and down every aisle, Jessica found some slimy, sticky plastic insects. She tried them out on the counter. When they were dropped, they stuck to glass in funny positions. They looked real, too.

"These are perfect for Sherrie. We'll scare her out of her wits," Jessica said, and Ellen laughed as her friend paid for the bugs.

"What'll we do with them?" Ellen asked. "We can't just throw them at her."

"No, I've got another idea. You know how Sherrie always carries that lozenge box around with her? She leaves it on the table next to her plate," Jessica said.

"Oh, yes," Ellen replied. "You want to fill the box with bugs?"

"Yes," said Jessica. Ellen followed her into a pharmacy, where Jessica purchased a box of the exact some brand of lozenges Sherrie used. "Well, we'll do this," Jessica leaned up against the wall of a building and proceeded to empty the lozenges out of the box into Ellen's hand. Then she filled the box with the sticky fake bugs. "We'll take away Sherrie's box when she's not looking and replace it with our box. The rest will be history."

"How will we do that?" Ellen wanted to know. "Won't she see us?"

"Not if she's busy talking or something," Jessica said. "I'll be talking to her and you can exchange the boxes."

"Thanks for the honor," Ellen replied, rolling her eyes. "I can't wait."

Eight

◇

On Saturday afternoon, Ms. MacDonald and Mr. Stefan took the whole choral group skating. There was ice skating on one level and roller skating on the other. When they got back to the hotel, Elizabeth and Anna asked Mrs. Isaacs if they could go for a walk. They promised not to go far.

"I suppose it would be all right. Just be back in time to change for dinner," she said.

"Oh, good, here's our big chance," Anna said excitedly. "If we're lucky, the Linwoods will be hanging around outside the embassy."

"Who hangs around outside an embassy?" Elizabeth asked, laughing. "Especially when the family is so important."

"You're right." Anna pulled on her jacket and they headed toward the elevators. "Well, maybe we'll catch a glimpse of them in their limousine or something."

It was cold outside but the sun was shining brightly. As they walked down Sixteenth Street, Elizabeth tried to figure out what flags were flying at the different embassies.

"Come on, Elizabeth. This is it," Anna said finally, tugging on Elizabeth's arm. Elizabeth followed her to the front gate of the Australian Embassy. Two guards stood by the door, dressed in navy blue uniforms. They looked very serious.

Anna went up to one of the guards and said, "Excuse me, can you tell me if there are any teenage girls named Leslie living here?"

"I don't know of any teenage girls in the embassy young lady, but perhaps you should ask someone else tomorrow. Tonight they're closing early to get ready for a big reception," the guard explained.

"A reception?" Anna asked eagerly. Her eyes lit up.

"Yes. We're welcoming our newest arrivals from Australia," the guard went on. "It starts at eight o'clock."

Anna turned to Elizabeth. "That has to be Leslie's family he's talking about!" Then she lowered her voice. "I have to go to that reception tonight!"

They thanked the guard and walked away from the embassy.

"I guess you could ask Mrs. Isaacs if it's OK with her," Elizabeth suggested.

"She'll say no," Anna stated gloomily.

"Well, how about telling her the truth about Leslie?" Elizabeth asked. "Maybe she'll be sympathetic and let you go."

"I doubt it. Mrs. Isaacs is so strict. She won't let anyone do anything," Anna replied. "She would probably get angry at me because I came to Washington just to see Leslie and not to sing."

"I don't think she would," Elizabeth said. "I think Mrs. Isaacs is nicer than you think."

"I don't want to find out, Elizabeth," Anna told her. "I just want to get into that embassy tonight. I guess now I'll just have to get a sore throat and go up to my room early."

Elizabeth knew what her friend was thinking, and she didn't like it one bit. "Anna, I don't think it's a good idea to leave the hotel without permission. You could get into a lot of trouble," Elizabeth warned. "I know how much you want to see Leslie, but there's got to be a better way. Why don't you let me talk to Mr. Stefan and Ms. McDonald? I'm sure they would let you go if they knew how important it was to you."

"You thought it was OK for me to get a sore throat so that I didn't have to sing," Anna reminded her. "What's so different about this?"

"Leaving the hotel without permission is what's different," Elizabeth said. "For one thing, you can get in a lot more trouble."

"It doesn't seem so different to me," Anna replied, sighing heavily. "Just promise me you won't say anything, OK? I don't want to take the chance of them saying no."

Elizabeth looked at her friend and sighed. "All right, I promise. But I still think you should talk to them. Maybe we can think of a safe way to get to the embassy before tonight."

When they got back to the hotel, Jessica was doing a headstand in the middle of their room. She landed on the floor with a thump. "Lizzie, Mr. Stefan wants to talk to you about the after-dinner singing tonight. He's in the Blue Room downstairs."

"OK, I'll go now," Elizabeth said. She hung up her coat and left the room.

Once Elizabeth had gone, Jessica turned to Anna. "So what's going on? What happened on your walk?"

Excitedly, Anna told her. "We found out there's a big reception at the Australian Embassy tonight. I'm going to go."

Jessica's eyes grew wide. "No kidding? How are you going to do that?"

Anna glanced around the room, then whispered, "Is anyone else here?"

"No, Mrs. Isaacs is downstairs getting her hair done," Jessica said. "And Ellen went with a bunch of kids to the souvenir shop. But you don't have to worry about her anyway," Jessica added. "Tell me."

"I'm thinking of sneaking out after dinner," Anna said in a low voice, but her tone was full of determination.

"Whoa, Anna, that's pretty dangerous," Jessica said. As the more adventurous Wakefield twin, she was usually up for any excitement. But this was a little different. They were so close to the actual competition, and Jessica was nervous about being disqualified if she was caught doing something wrong. Putting plastic insects in a lozenge box was one thing, but sneaking out was another story. "Did you tell Elizabeth?" she asked.

"Yes," Anna admitted. "But I made her promise not to talk to Mrs. Isaacs or anyone else about trying to get permission."

"You could get in a lot of trouble for sneaking out," Jessica said.

"But, Jessica! This is my only chance to meet Leslie!" Anna cried. "Why don't you come with me? It will be a great big party, too. I know just what I'm going to wear! Come with me!"

Jessica loved parties more than anything. She also loved big glamorous occasions, and a reception at the Australian Embassy certainly would be exciting. She'd never get an opportunity to do anything quite this grown-up in Sweet Valley.

"Imagine! All those foreign ambassadors. And the women will all have on beautiful dresses!" Jessica closed her eyes and breathed deeply as she imagined the scene, with herself in the center of it all. Anna's voice brought her back to reality.

"Well? What do you think?" Anna persisted. "Do you want to come or not?"

Jessica sighed and nodded. "OK, but we have to have a plan." She rested her chin in her hand for a minute and thought. Then she said, "I know. Your laryngitis is going to turn into a terrible sore throat so you have to go to bed right after dinner. I'll bring you upstairs and get you hot tea and lemon, stuff like that. Then, at eight-thirty, the choral groups are supposed to sing carols for the hotel visitors in one of the lounges. While everyone's downstairs singing, we'll sneak out."

"But how? How are we going to get through the lobby without being seen?" Anna wanted to know.

Jessica remembered seeing a tea trolley being taken down the hall to another elevator.

"We'll use the service elevator," she told Anna triumphantly. Suddenly, Jessica wasn't worried about getting caught anymore. She was certain the plan would work. And she couldn't wait to put it into action.

Nine

◇

Elizabeth, Jessica, Ellen and Anna sat together at dinner that evening. Since her meeting that afternoon with Mr. Stefan, Elizabeth had been thinking about the choral performance to take place after dinner. Mr. Stefan had asked her to lead the Sweet Valley group in the singing, which was a real honor. She couldn't wait for dinner to be over! She had also asked Mr. Stefan if they could go caroling outside after the hotel presentation and he had said yes!

She hadn't seen Anna and Jessica since her meeting with Mr. Stefan, so she hadn't told them yet about the singing. "This means we can get out of the hotel afterward and go caroling in the area. We can even go to the embassy," Elizabeth explained excitedly.

Anna and Jessica exchanged glances. "You

don't think they're going to invite a whole bunch of carolers into the embassy, do you?" asked Jessica. "That's crazy."

"They might ask us in, especially if Anna's with us," Elizabeth suggested hopefully. "What do you think, Anna?"

"I-I don't know, Elizabeth," Anna stammered, looking at Jessica.

"But Anna—" Elizabeth began. Jessica cut her off.

"Shhh! Look who's here," Jessica said, nodding toward Sherrie, who had just sat down directly across from them.

Sherrie placed her lozenge box on the table and turned to talk to one of her friends. Ellen quickly made her move, she slipped the box soundlessly off the table and into her pocket. Then she replaced it with the joke lozenge box and moved a few feet away.

Across the table, Elizabeth continued to eat. Next to her, Jessica seemed very nervous. She kept fidgeting in her seat. She didn't touch her food, either.

"Jess, are you OK?" Elizabeth finally asked, concerned. "You're not eating."

"I'm not very hungry," she replied, unable to keep her eyes off Sherrie.

Now Sherrie was talking to the boy next to her. Elizabeth looked at her closely. Maybe Sherrie was the reason Jessica was nervous. But Elizabeth was nervous, too, because she didn't know what

Anna planned to do about the embassy. She wished she could talk to Anna privately. Maybe when dinner was over there would be an opportunity.

Absently, Sherrie reached for her lozenge box. She opened it without looking inside, then tilted the box to get one out.

"Aaah!" Sherrie screamed, pushing the lozenge box onto the floor. It fell with a tinny crash and the small rubbery insects fell out. Sherrie kept screaming and jumping around.

Knives and forks clattered onto plates, and some of her schoolmates rushed over to see what had happened. Girls and boys nearby started to scream, too. Sherrie was standing up, staring at the floor in horror.

"Someone has played a joke on me!" she wailed. "They put those horrible bugs in my lozenge box! I know it was those Sweet Valley girls! I just know it! Anna and Jessica! It had to be them!"

"Sit down and try to be calm!" one of the chaperones told Sherrie.

"I don't want to sit down! Something else might happen!" she cried.

Some boys sitting nearby laughed. "It's not funny!" Sherrie shrieked. "Those girls should be punished."

She looked around wildly and focused on Elizabeth. Everyone else turned to stare at Elizabeth, too. "Why are you looking at me?" Elizabeth asked, and then it dawned on her. Of course! They must all think she was Jessica! Elizabeth turned and saw that her twin was no longer sitting next to her. Anna was gone, too. Where were they? Seconds ago, the three girls had been sitting together. Elizabeth scanned the dining room, but they had vanished!

One of the Grant chaperones, approached Elizabeth. "Young lady, is this true?"

"No!" cried Elizabeth. "I didn't know anything about it."

"What about your sister and your friends?" the chaperone persisted.

"I'm sure they would never do such an awful thing," Elizabeth claimed. "There's been a big mistake. It had to be somebody else."

"What a lie!" huffed Sherrie, her eyes flashing. "You're Jessica, and you and Anna did it. You're just covering up for Anna, as usual. Otherwise, why would Anna disappear?"

Suddenly, Elizabeth remembered what Anna had said earlier about getting a sore throat. She didn't think it was right for Anna to lie in order to sneak out. But right now, Elizabeth needed a good explanation for why her friend and her sister were not at the dinner table. She was sure they were up to something, but she had to protect them. "Jessica probably took Anna up to her room because she was complaining of a sore throat. You'll see, she'll be back down here later."

"Hey, wait a minute!" Ellen put in. She had heard what was going on and came to Elizabeth's rescue. "Sherrie, this is Elizabeth. Not Jessica."

Ellen continued, "Jessica took Anna up to her room because Anna's sick. She can barely talk tonight."

"Oh, sure," grumbled Sherrie.

"Elizabeth—you *are* Elizabeth, aren't you?" Mrs. Isaacs asked her as she approached the table.

"Yes, Mrs. Isaacs," Elizabeth replied.

"I suggest you stay here while I go looking for Anna and Jessica. They must apologize for this," Mrs. Isaacs insisted.

"But you don't know if they actually did anything!" Elizabeth cried.

"Well, I'm going to find out if they did," Mrs. Isaacs answered in a huff. "We can't have our Sweet Valley girls playing pranks like this."

Sherrie shot Elizabeth a poisonous look, then turned and went back to her seat.

Elizabeth was devastated. She was sure Jessica had pulled the prank. And now Mrs. Isaacs and everybody else would know about it. Jessica might be kicked out of the competition. And what was worse, now Jessica and Anna had disappeared and were probably going to be in more serious trouble! Elizabeth sighed heavily. She just hoped Jessica had taken Anna up to her room as she had said.

"I wonder where Anna and Jessica really

went," Ellen said in a low voice. "Do you know where they are?"

"No," Elizabeth said. "But I sure wish I did. Jessica has a solo in the performance later. I hope Mrs. Isaacs finds them before the music starts."

But knowing how much Anna wanted to go to the embassy reception, Elizabeth was worried. She was almost certain now that Jessica was helping Anna to sneak out. It was the kind of adventure Jessica loved.

"Quick! There's an elevator!" Anna whispered, yanking Jessica by the arm and pulling her into the waiting elevator. They had exited the dining room just as Sherrie had started carrying on.

The elevator lurched to a stop on their floor and the two girls stepped out and ran down the hall to their room. While they were changing into party dresses, Anna said, "You know, that was a super idea with the lozenge box, Jessica. And it happened just at the right time. You couldn't have planned it better!"

"Yes, I know," Jessica replied, quite pleased with herself. "I'm glad she found the bugs before we left. I almost forgot all about them. But it sure gave us a perfect way out of there. I bet they still don't know we're missing."

"We can't be sure," said Anna. "We'd better hurry."

At last, they were dressed. Cautiously, they

scanned the hall to see if anyone was around, then sneaked to the service elevator.

The doors opened to reveal a janitor with a laundry cart inside. He looked at the girls with suspicion. "Hey, why are you girls here?" he demanded. "There's another elevator for hotel guests, you know. You shouldn't be using this one."

Jessica and Anna looked at each other. "Sorry. We thought *this* was the only elevator. Thanks for telling us," Jessica said.

"Are you sure you girls know what you're doing?" the man demanded.

"Yes," said Jessica firmly, as she took Anna by the hand and backed away from the elevator. As soon as the doors closed, they headed for the staircase. "Do you think he'll say anything to anybody?" Anna asked.

"Who knows? But we can't worry about him now," Jessica replied.

Just as they reached the stairwell, Jessica froze. The door to the passenger elevator at the end of the hall opened, and out stepped Mrs. Isaacs! Anna's hand went cold in hers. They stood there, unable to move. Amazingly, the chaperone didn't seem to be looking at them at all! She was looking for something in her purse.

Jessica held tightly to Anna's hand, leading her down the stairs. The rustle of their taffeta and silk dresses echoed in the stairwell. They took their shoes off so that no one would hear them running down the stairs.

Breathless, they reached the ground floor.

Jessica looked around, hoping no one would notice them. But they had nothing to worry about, because the lobby was quite full.

"We should just make a run for it," Anna suggested, peering over Jessica's shoulder.

"If we run, everyone's going to notice us," Jessica said. "I think we should walk out, then run once we get to the street."

"OK."

They put their shoes back on, and taking a deep breath, the two girls walked quickly through the lobby, looking neither right nor left. Once they reached the red carpet leading out of the hotel, they broke into a run.

Halfway down the block, Jessica started laughing. "We did it! We did it!" she cried, hugging Anna.

Sherrie Dunston just happened to step out of the elevator at the exact instant that Jessica and Anna dashed out of the hotel. Sherrie noticed the hems of Jessica's red silk dress and Anna's pale blue taffeta dress sticking out below their winter coats. They were *not* the same dresses that they were wearing at dinner. *They must be on their way to meet some boys, all dressed up like that,* Sherrie decided. This was certainly juicy news. She couldn't wait to find someone to tell this bit of information to.

Ms. McDonald, the Sweet Valley music teacher, came into the lobby. Sherrie approached her, smiling.

"Hi, Ms. McDonald. I'm Sherrie Dunston," she said.

"Hello, Sherrie." Ms. McDonald replied.

"I just wanted to let you know that I just saw two of your singers leave the hotel. They were all dressed up, and I heard them say they were going to meet some boys," Sherrie said coyly.

Ms. McDonald's expression became stern. "Oh, really?"

"Yes." Sherrie enjoyed the way the teacher's face had changed when she heard the word "boys." Of course, she had made that up, but it was a good story!

"Which two Sweet Valley girls did you see, Sherrie?" Ms. McDonald asked.

"Jessica and Anna," replied Sherrie. "The two girls everyone was looking for at dinner."

Of course, the teacher had been in the dining room and knew the story of Sherrie's lozenge box and the missing girls.

"Thank you for telling me, Sherrie," said Ms. McDonald, walking quickly toward the dining room door.

Sherrie followed the teacher and watched her go over to Elizabeth and start questioning her.

"What do you know about your sister's plans for this evening, Elizabeth?" Ms. McDonald asked.

"Nothing, Ms. McDonald," Elizabeth replied.

"Well, it appears that she and Anna left in order to meet some boys," Ms. McDonald told her.

Elizabeth's mouth dropped open. Sherrie sneaked out of the room quickly before anyone could see her smiling.

Ten

◇

The Australian Embassy looked dazzling. Jessica thought it looked like a fairy-tale castle decorated for the holiday. Heavy red curtains framed each window. Twinkling party lights were strung around the entrance and on the trees outside, and huge wreaths hung on the doors. Even the door-men were dressed in red uniforms. A group of beautifully dressed people stood waiting to get in-side.

Jessica and Anna watched in awe as sleek lim-ousines lined up outside the embassy. Elegant men and women got out of the cars and glided up to the front entrance.

"They are all so gorgeous," Jessica said in a hushed voice. She was mesmerized by all the fur coats and glittering jewelry. "They must be the most important people in the whole world!"

She closed her eyes and imagined herself walking into the embassy, head held high as though she was some kind of royalty. She saw herself wearing a fur coat and high heels and beautiful jewelry. She knew she could pull it off, too. She could look older when she wanted to. People would stop and say, "Who is that pretty girl?"

"Jessica, the guests all seem to know someone or have an invitation," Anna noted. "How will we get in?"

Jessica stopped daydreaming and thought for a minute. Everyone did either carry an invitation or else seemed to know the doormen and were just being let in. Children followed their parents into the building.

"Simple, Anna," Jessica answered. "Look, kids are invited, too. That makes us less noticeable. All we have to do is look like we belong to some important family. We can pretend we're the daughters of one of these couples."

"Great idea!" exclaimed Anna. A family was just entering the embassy as they were talking. Next a tall, handsome man and his black-haired wife started up the steps. They didn't seem have any children with them.

"There—those two will do," Jessica said. "We'll be their instant family. Keep your fingers crossed." Anna ran alongside her, giggling. "Now it's my turn to adopt parents."

The girls fell into step behind the couple. "Oh, hello, Mr. and Mrs. Davis. How are you . . . ?" people all around them kept asking the distinguished-looking pair. The girls smiled as though they knew everyone, and everyone smiled back at them. Their "parents" smiled at them, too, almost as though they were really related! The plan was working!

Inside the embassy, Anna took a deep breath. She could hardly believe they had made it. Now she would meet her sister at last!

She scanned the room, taking in the high ceiling with its massive chandelier. People dressed in formal clothes stood in clusters, talking. A Christmas tree filled one corner, and the room smelled of woodsmoke, pine and perfume.

Anna was so excited she could hardly stand still. She wondered where her sister might be. Leslie could be anywhere in this room, just inches from her, at this very moment!

She couldn't stand the suspense any longer. She tapped a lady on the shoulder.

"Excuse me. Could you tell me where the Linwoods are?"

"Yes, dear. Mr. and Mrs. Linwood are right over there, next to the fireplace," the lady said. "I think their children are here, too."

Jessica and Anna turned and stared at the distinguished, dark-haired man and the tall woman whose pale blond hair was twisted into a bun. The firelight danced in their hair and made a sort of halo around them.

"I guess they're almost related to me, too," Anna said thoughtfully.

"Do you want to introduce yourself?" Jessica asked.

"No, I want to find my sister first," Anna replied. "She's more important right now."

"Look over there, by the tree," Jessica said. There were kids of all ages milling about near the huge Christmas tree. Presents were piled high under the evergreen branches. A handsome teenage boy was helping a little girl fix the sail on a toy boat. But there was no one who looked like she could be Leslie.

Someone passed by with a tray of delicious-looking hors d'oeuvres. Near the kitchen, there was a trolley full of rich desserts.

"Boy, I've never seen anything like this!" Anna exclaimed in wonder. "Imagine, my long-lost sister lives like this all the time."

"Maybe not all the time," Jessica corrected her. "This is a special occasion, remember? I'm sure these people's kids eat hamburgers and hot dogs just like everybody else."

"But they probably always get chocolate mousse for dessert," Anna said, giggling. "Let's go upstairs. Maybe I'll find my sister up there."

"We have to get past those guards first," said Jessica, eyeing the two uniformed men standing at the foot of the stairs. "I know. We can just talk as though we're friends of Leslie's."

"OK." The two girls kept up a steady chatter

as they walked past the guards. "Oh, I just love your new dress, Anna," Jessica remarked in a loud voice so that the guards would be sure to hear her. "And I'll bet Leslie will like it, too." "I'm glad you like it," Anna replied. "I can't wait to show it to Leslie."

The guards didn't bat an eyelash as the girls sailed right past them and up the stairs.

The two girls giggled. "It worked!" Jessica whispered. "OK, let's check all the rooms. We can start at this end of the hall and work down."

They did exactly that, tiptoeing from one room to the next, looking for Anna's sister. No one seemed to be around.

"None of these rooms look like a teenager lives in them," Anna commented.

Jessica laughed. "Maybe they don't allow rock posters on the walls and blasting stereos in embassies."

"Maybe," Anna replied. "Or maybe Leslie's family isn't going to live at the embassy. Maybe they'll get a house somewhere else."

They entered a room with a dartboard on the wall and a pool table in the center.

"Hey, a game room," Anna exclaimed, running her hand over the green felt of the pool table.

"It looks like a good place for kids to hang out," observed Jessica. "Let's remember this room."

Then they went into another room and Anna opened a door, thinking she would find a closet. It turned out to be the door to an adjoining room. She pulled it open and peered inside.

"Jessica! Come here," she cried. Jessica hurried over to her side. It was an office or study, lined with bookshelves, with a big desk in the center of the room. The room smelled of leather and pipe tobacco.

"It looks important," Jessica said. "I wonder if this is where Leslie's father will be working."

"It seems like a secret office. I mean, why do you have to go through that room to get to this room?" questioned Anna.

Jessica shrugged. "I don't know. It would be easy to get lost in a place like this."

The two girls stepped into the room. Just then, Anna grabbed Jessica's arm. "Shhh! I heard something!"

There was a noise just outside the hall door.

"What do we do now?" Anna whispered, panic-stricken.

Then Jessica saw the door inch open. Instantly, she yanked Anna down behind an ornate Victorian screen which hid a bank of file cabinets. The girls crouched behind the screen as far as they could get and held their breath. Seconds later, a man stepped into the room.

Eleven

◇

Back at the hotel, Elizabeth sat in the dining room, feeling more and more miserable. Mrs. Isaacs came in to report that Jessica and Anna were not in their rooms. And Mr. Stefan said that because the girls were missing, there would be no evening music presentation by the Sweet Valley Choral Group. Not to mention the fact that there would be no caroling afterward.

Ms. McDonald sat across from Elizabeth, asking questions.

"Ms. McDonald, I don't think you should believe Sherrie's story," Elizabeth pleaded. "I'm sure she doesn't know anything and just wants to get Jessica and Anna in trouble. I know my sister wouldn't be out with boys. She knows the rules."

"Nevertheless, Elizabeth, your sister and Anna appear to have left this hotel. That is breaking the rules right there," Ms. McDonald told her sternly. "And that is very serious. We have no idea where the two girls may have gone. I have to admit, I'm a little worried."

Mr. Stefan came over to their table. "That's right, Elizabeth. As far as we know, we have two young girls missing in Washington at night. They don't know their way around this big city. If they don't show up in the next five minutes, we'll be forced to call the police."

"No!" Elizabeth blurted out, clapping her hands to her face in horror.

"What's wrong, Elizabeth?" Mr. Stefan demanded. "Don't you think your parents would want us to find Jessica?"

"Of course, that's not it. It's just . . ." Elizabeth was really scared now. She hadn't forgotten her promise to Anna, but she didn't think she could keep that promise any longer. She felt that she had no choice but to tell Mr. Stefan and Ms. McDonald about the Australian Embassy. Otherwise, Jessica and Anna were going to be in more serious trouble. What if the police were called and they came charging over to the hotel? How embarrassing that would be—for everyone. And unless she told the truth, that was exactly what would happen.

"I'm pretty sure I know where they are," Elizabeth finally said.

"Oh?" Mr. Stefan and Ms. McDonald eyed her with curiosity. "Where are they?"

"At the Australian Embassy," replied Elizabeth.

"Did I hear you right? Did you say the *Australian Embassy*?" Mr. Stefan boomed. His voice could be very loud when he wanted it to be.

"Yes, that's right," replied Elizabeth. "It's not far from here."

"Why in the world did they go there? Is Anna Australian?" Mr. Stefan asked.

"No. They went there because they're looking for someone Anna knows," Elizabeth explained. "A long-lost relative." She decided not to tell the whole story. She wanted to keep at least part of her promise to Anna.

Seeing that Elizabeth was getting quite a lot of attention, Sherrie marched past the table so she could listen.

"Why didn't Anna simply ask for permission to visit this person?" questioned Ms. McDonald. "Why all this secrecy?"

"Because she was afraid you would both say no," Elizabeth said. "There's a big party going on at the embassy tonight to honor the people she went to see. They're pretty important people."

"Do her parents know that she planned to visit these relatives?" asked Mr. Stefan.

"Well, no, but they knew the family would be in Washington," said Elizabeth.

It was difficult to tell the story without telling the whole truth, especially with Sherrie standing there smirking.

"Don't you think Elizabeth should be punished for withholding information?" Sherrie asked Ms. McDonald. "She's caused a lot of trouble."

"We'll worry about that, Sherrie," Ms. Mc-Donald said stiffly.

"All three of them should be kicked out of the competition," Sherrie declared. "Our instructors would kick them out and send them home in a minute!"

Elizabeth glared at Sherrie.

"Sherrie, we'll handle this, thank you," Ms. McDonald said, through gritted teeth.

Mrs. Isaacs came into the room just then, and Ms. McDonald relayed Elizabeth's story.

"This is terrible! Why didn't the girls say something to us?" cried Mrs. Isaacs, clapping her hands together. "That settles it. Elizabeth, you are to go to your room to wait. I'm going to the embassy myself to find the girls."

"I'll go with you," Mr. Stefan offered.

"Can't you just wait until they get back?" Elizabeth asked. "I know they're safe. They'll be back soon."

"Elizabeth, they're our responsibility and we must make sure they're all right," Mr. Stefan explained.

"That's right," Ms. McDonald agreed. "I'll stay here and hold down the fort."

"Can't I come, too? To help you look?" Elizabeth pleaded. "I'm sure I can help."

"I want you to stay here," Mrs. Isaacs said. "Just in case the girls call."

Elizabeth was angry. It didn't seem fair that she should have to stay behind.

From their hiding place, Jessica and Anna watched a man dressed in a tuxedo enter the room. He was small, with dark curly hair and he wore glasses. Obviously he was a guest from the party downstairs. He looked behind the door and the couch as if he thought someone would be in the room.

He must've heard us, Jessica thought to herself. He looked very nervous, as though he didn't really belong there. And he kept looking toward the door as if he was worried about being discovered!

Behind the screen, the two girls held their breath. The man crossed the floor to the massive antique desk in the center of the room. He was not even five feet away from them! He was so close that Jessica could make out a huge diamond ring on the little finger of his left hand. It flashed as he started going through the drawers, riffling papers. Then he pulled out a couple of sheets of paper and examined them. He held the sheets up to the light. Then he folded them quickly, looking around as though he wanted to make sure no one had seen him. He stuffed them into the pocket of his tuxedo and went through more drawers.

As Jessica watched, it occurred to her that if

the man didn't find what he wanted in the desk, he might try the file cabinets next. They had to get out of there. But how?

Tapping Anna to get her attention, she pointed at the file cabinets and mouthed the words, "He's going to look here next. We've got to get out."

Just then someone else tapped Anna's shoulder. She nearly started to scream, but Jessica covered her mouth with her hand. Jessica practically jumped out of her skin when she turned around and saw a boy half-hidden by the cabinets. The two girls crouched in their hiding place, too terrified to move. They both recognized him—he was the cute teenage boy they'd seen downstairs by the Christmas tree.

He put his finger over his lips, motioning for them to keep quiet. Then he pointed to an open panel in the wall behind them. Jessica wondered how he could have possibly gotten the panel open without making any noise. But there wasn't time to find out. He motioned them to follow him.

Both Jessica and Anna looked from the man to the boy. They really had no choice. They had to trust the boy. Silently, he slipped through the open panel. Anna and Jessica followed, moving into the dark tunnel.

Suddenly, they heard the man growl, "Hey, stop!"

Jessica was just pulling the panel shut behind her when his hand came through the panel and tried to yank it open! Terrified, she tugged as hard as she could. But he was too strong for her. After a brief struggle, she let go and followed the others down the long, dark corridor. All three of them were hunched over because there wasn't room in the corridor to stand up straight.

"He's right behind us," Jessica whispered to the others.

"Hurry!" the boy whispered back.

Jessica shivered uncontrollably. She could hear the man's heavy breathing behind her. "Stop!" he shouted, and his voice echoed off the walls eerily.

The corridor was like a tunnel, and the boy seemed to know it by heart. There were other corridors off the main one, but the three children stayed in the main one until they reached another panel in a wall.

Jessica imagined she felt the man's breath right on her neck. She was certain that any minute he was going to reach out and grab her!

After what seemed like forever, the boy pulled open the panel. Anna, Jessica and the boy climbed out into a huge, brightly lit room, decorated with chandeliers and plush Oriental rugs. A gigantic marble fireplace was at one end.

"This is called the Light Room," the boy explained. "The previous ambassador collected chandeliers." The chandeliers made diamonds of light dance on the walls.

Jessica pulled the panel closed. It was a relief

not to hear that heavy breathing behind her. Then she noticed how good-looking the boy really was. He was tall and had curly red hair, blue eyes and lots of freckles.

"Thanks for rescuing us," Anna whispered gratefully.

"You're not safe yet," the boy told her, his face serious. "Come on, follow me. We have to hurry. That man isn't far behind us."

He crossed the room and led them through another room, then another. "Where are we?" cried Jessica. "I hear footsteps in the next room!" Anna whispered, her face full of terror. "How did he get out of the secret passage so fast?"

"Hurry!" the boy urged, and he sprang ahead into the next room, which was a nursery.

There were bunk beds set up in one corner, a crib in another. Stuffed animals were arranged in the crib, and it looked like a baby had recently occupied the room. Anna stumbled over a toy that was on the floor and it let out a loud squeak. Jessica gasped.

"Shhh!" the boy warned. He climbed up the ladder to the top bunk and then pushed at the ceiling.

"What are you doing?" asked Anna.

"This is a trap door that leads to the attic. I don't think he'll find us up here."

Suddenly, the trap door budged and the boy was able to push it upward. Then he climbed through the opening.

He turned around to offer a hand to Jessica and Anna. Once both girls were safely through the opening, the boy shut it and bolted it from the inside.

Just as he pushed the bolt into place, they heard the man enter the nursery and curse. "Where are you? You can't get away from me, you rotten kids!"

Then the man stepped on the squeaky toy and it let out a loud noise. Jessica, Anna and the boy had to put their hands over their mouths to keep from giggling.

"I wonder what he's after." Jessica whispered. "Is he a spy?"

"He's definitely a spy," the boy explained in a low voice. "I saw him come upstairs so I followed him. I sneaked into the secret passage so I could watch him from a safe place. He must have been looking for some important documents in my father's desk."

"He did find some papers in that desk!" Jessica exclaimed, still careful to whisper so the spy wouldn't hear her.

"Oh, no. Those papers could be dangerous in his hands," the boy said. "We have to stop him from leaving the building with them."

"I bet he's not going to hang around all these people," Anna said. "He's going to try to get out as fast as he can."

"We'll have to check all the exits," Jessica suggested.

The boy smiled at her. "Good idea. I'll tell my father. He'll know exactly what to do."

Finally, the noise below them stopped. Jessica heard the footsteps travel away from the nursery. The boy unbolted the trap door, looked around cautiously and then they let themselves out.

Downstairs, the party was in full swing. The two girls followed the boy right over to his father, who was standing next to a man Jessica was sure she'd seen on television!

"Who's that?" Jessica asked Anna. "I know I've seen that face on TV."

"A newsman, maybe," Anna suggested. "He looks familiar to me, too."

Watching the boy talking to his father, Anna realized who the boy's father was. She cried out, "That's Mr. Linwood! Leslie's father! We saw him when we came in, remember? This boy must be Leslie's brother, Jessica!"

"Look, Mr. Linwood is just about to give a speech, Anna," Jessica pointed out. "There's no time to talk about your sister now."

Sure enough, Mr. Linwood stepped onto a small platform and said, "May I have your attention, please! I'm sorry for this inconvenience, but we are having all the exits sealed off at this time. This should last only about fifteen minutes, and we'll be sure to announce when the exits are open again. Please be assured that everything is under control. I hope you all will continue to enjoy the party. Thank you."

Mr. Linwood came over to Jessica and Anna. "Thank you both for helping my son," he said, smiling. "But now I'll need some help from you to find this spy. You're the only ones who know what he looks like."

"I'd know him anywhere," Jessica announced proudly.

"Actually, he's kind of ordinary-looking," Anna said. "He doesn't look like a spy."

"Nobody looks like a spy," Jessica replied knowledgeably. "Unless he's wearing a trench coat."

Mr. Linwood laughed.

Jessica thought she would remember what the spy looked like for the rest of her life. Anna described him—short, with curly dark hair. He also had tiny brown eyes and wore glasses. Jessica stared at all the short, male guests until they looked a little uncomfortable. She even looked to see if any of them appeared to have papers in their tuxedo pockets.

"He's probably wearing a disguise," Jessica said.

"Yeah, he could be," the boy agreed. "Maybe we should check out the rooms downstairs."

Jessica, Anna and the boy made a search of all the downstairs rooms, studying all the guests closely. They didn't find anyone who looked like the spy.

"How about the kitchen?" Mrs. Linwood suggested. "That's the only room left."

Jessica marched ahead of the others, certain that she would recognize the spy. But no one in the kitchen looked like the man who had chased them.

Then the chef walked in carrying a turkey on a big tray. He was small, but he had a bushy beard and mustache. He didn't wear glasses, either, just a tall chef's hat and a white apron. *That's not him either,* Jessica thought.

But then she noticed something else. The chef wore a ring on his finger. It was the same diamond ring she had noticed on the spy's finger! She knew she was right—she always noticed valuable things!

She pointed her finger at him. "That's him!" she cried.

The boy looked at her in horror. "It can't be! That's the chef!" he exclaimed.

"No, he's not! He's the spy!" Jessica insisted.

The chef stared at her, wide-eyed. Then with one quick movement he threw the tray with the turkey on it toward her. Jessica dodged out of the way. The turkey fell on the floor. Juice and stuffing splashed over everyone—including Jessica. The chef lunged for the swinging kitchen doors.

"I can't believe you've ruined my dress!" Jessica cried, gazing down at the splotches of grease.

Mr. Linwood came rushing through the swinging doors leading into the kitchen, and ran smack into the chef. The chef pushed him out of the way and made another run for the doors.

"That's him! The chef is your spy! Grab him!"

cried Anna, pointing at the man, whose hat was falling off.

Two guards burst through the doorway and grabbed the chef. He struggled with them for a few minutes, but he couldn't get away.

Mr. Linwood walked over to the man and studied his face closely. "Why, you're not Oscar," he said in surprise.

"Oscar didn't show up today," explained one of the waiters. "This man said he was the replacement."

The spy glared at Mr. Linwood and the children as the guards placed handcuffs on him. Then the guards frisked him. As he was leaning over, Jessica noticed some papers sticking out of the top of his socks!

"Look there!" she shouted, pointing at the papers.

Sure enough, the documents he had taken from the desk were rolled up and stuffed into his socks.

One of the guards handed the documents to Mr. Linwood. Mr. Linwood thanked him and looked closely at the man.

"You thought you'd get away with this, did you?" Mr. Linwood asked. "Well, you're not as smart as you think you are. And thanks to these three young people, you're not going to do any more damage for a long time."

A cheer rose from all the people in the kitchen as the spy was led away.

One of the waiters said, "You know, I told him he was taking the turkey out much too early, but he didn't listen to me."

Everyone laughed.

"Well, I'm glad *he's* not doing the cooking," another waiter said.

Some of the workers got busy cleaning the turkey off the floor.

"It's not like Oscar not to call in," Mr. Linwood said. "I have a feeling he's here somewhere."

A couple of waiters went in search of him and brought him back a few minutes later. He looked frightened to death.

"Mr. Linwood, we found him in the linen closet, tied up with his own apron and gagged with a dishrag," one of the waiters announced.

"Poor Oscar!" cried Mr. Linwood, leading the chef into the next room.

"Who would've guessed we'd get to help capture a real live spy!" Jessica exclaimed. "Isn't this exciting?"

"Now that it's all over, it's very exciting," Mr. Linwood's son told her, smiling. "I'm glad you both were here to help."

Jessica and Anna laughed happily.

"This probably happens to you all the time," said Jessica admiringly.

"No way," the boy said, shaking his head. "Things were dull until you got here."

Jessica blushed in spite of herself.

Outside, they could hear all the police sirens heading toward the embassy. Jessica and Anna hugged each other, relieved that the spy had been caught.

Twelve

◇

Elizabeth was curled up on the bed in her hotel room, trying to read a book. But she couldn't concentrate at all. She couldn't stop thinking about Jessica and Anna. If Mr. Stefan and Mrs. Isaacs had found them, then they would be in big trouble. And if they hadn't been found . . . Why hadn't someone phoned to let her know what was going on? Elizabeth wondered.

Suddenly, there was a knock at the door. Elizabeth jumped up to answer it. Ellen stood outside holding a tray with a silver covered dish on it.

"Sorry to disappoint you. I know you were hoping to see Jessica and Anna," Ellen said. "I brought you some food."

"Thanks," Elizabeth said appreciatively. It seemed strange that Ellen was being so nice to her.

Ellen was one of Jessica's snobby, boy-crazy friends from the Unicorn Club and she and Elizabeth didn't have much in common. But for the moment things were different. She and Ellen were both worried about Jessica and Anna.

"Have you heard anything?" Elizabeth asked.

Ellen sat down in a chair. "No. All I know is what you know. Mr. Stefan and Mrs. Isaacs took a cab over to the embassy. No one has called here?"

"No," Elizabeth said, sighing. "I wish Mrs. Isaacs had let me go with them."

"Want anything to eat?" Ellen asked, lifting the cover off the silver dish. "I know you didn't get much dinner."

Elizabeth glanced at the dish and giggled. Ellen had brought some cake and cookies from the dessert tray.

"Oooh! Those look delicious!" Elizabeth cried, tasting a chocolate cookie. "This might be the best dinner I ever had."

"I caught Sherrie Dunston filling her bag with them," said Ellen. "I told her not to take one more or I was going to tell on her for stealing. She got out of there fast and left the rest for me."

Elizabeth giggled.

"Did you hear what Sherrie said to Ms. McDonald about Jessica and Anna meeting some boys?" she asked Ellen.

"Yes. I've never seen Ms. McDonald so angry," Ellen answered, biting into a piece of cake. "But don't worry. After they get to the embassy,

I'm sure none of the teachers will believe Sherrie's silly story."

Suddenly, Elizabeth said, "Did they decide whether there would be singing tonight?"

"Uh-huh. Sweet Valley's not singing, but Sherrie's doing a solo for Grant," reported Ellen. "And the whole Grant chorus is doing a big piece."

"Then everyone will see how great they are and nobody will know how super we are," Elizabeth said sadly. "I wish Anna and Jessica had listened to me. I don't think they had to get into all this trouble to get to the embassy." She told Ellen her idea about the caroling.

"Well, cheer up," Ellen said. "The good news is that tonight's performance doesn't count. We can save ourselves for the competition."

Elizabeth nodded. She hoped Ellen was right. She picked up another cookie and took a small bite. "I guess all we can do now is wait."

In spite of all the excitement about the spy, Anna did not forget the reason that she had come to Washington in the first place. It just seemed very hard to find the right time to talk to the Linwoods' son about his family. She waited until the spy was taken away, and then she decided to ask him about his sister.

But then there was an announcement that some gifts were about to be placed under the Christmas tree. "All children please come to the Christmas tree!" someone shouted.

Jessica, Anna and the boy went to stand over by the tree. Photographers pushed through the crowd to take pictures of the tree and the children. While they were watching the little kids bring up the presents, Jessica asked, "When do they open the gifts?"

"They're not going to," the boy said. "The presents aren't for these children. Every year the embassy collects gifts for needy children all over the world. Every kid who's invited to this party brings a gift for a needy child in a foreign country. It's usually something that will be useful to someone living in that country. The kids put the presents under the tree, and after the party the gifts are sent all around the world."

"How do they know what kinds of things to buy?" asked Jessica.

"When you pick the name of your recipient, the country is named on the same tag, along with a list of sample gifts," the boy explained.

"It sounds like a great idea," said Anna. She gazed at the brightly-colored presents under the tree. "You know, the one thing I really want for Christmas is to meet my sister."

"*Meet* your sister?" the boy looked at her strangely.

"Yes," she replied wistfully. "You know, we ran all the way through the embassy with you before I figured out who you are."

The boy smiled. "You've heard of my father, I guess."

"Yes. But it's not what you think. You have a sister, don't you?" Anna asked.

"Yes, I do," the boy answered, looking a little surprised.

Anna gasped. "I knew it! She's my long-lost sister! That's why I came all the way to Washington!"

The boy gazed at her in amazement. "Are you kidding me? My sister is two years old. She can't be your sister. Can she?"

"Your sister is a lot older than two, isn't she?" Jessica put in.

Anna was crushed. "Two? She's not supposed to be two. She's thirteen. What's this sister's name?"

"Jennifer."

"A-are you sure there isn't another Linwood family then? I mean, I know my sister's part of the Linwood family. Her name is Leslie Linwood, and her father was coming here from Australia." Suddenly, Anna burst into tears.

"Leslie?" the boy asked, looking a little baffled. "*I'm* Leslie Linwood. Could you be related to me?"

Anna looked up from her handkerchief and studied his face. Suddenly she saw him differently. Of course! She hadn't noticed it before, but now she saw how similar they looked. Leslie Linwood had the same shade of red, curly hair, the same blue eyes, even the same freckles as she did!

"Do you mean you could be my brother?" she exclaimed.

Jessica jumped up and down in excitement. "A brother instead of a sister? Oh, Anna, how exciting!" A waiter passed with a tray of tiny fruit tarts, and Jessica popped one into her mouth.

"We sure look enough alike to be brother and sister," Leslie said, looking at Anna closely. "Were you adopted?"

"Yes, were you?"

"Yes! But I didn't know that I had a sister!"

"I didn't know until last month, either," Anna replied. "I found a letter my parents had received from your parents. I was so shocked. My parents never told me about you. Then I decided I had to find you, er, my 'sister.'" She giggled. "I guess I just thought with a name like Leslie that you'd be a girl."

"Surprise, surprise," he said, giving her a big hug. "Nice to meet you, Sister."

Thirteen

◇

At that moment, Mr. and Mrs. Linwood came over to talk to the children.

"I don't believe we've met," Mrs. Linwood said, extending her hand to the two girls.

"Well, they seem to have gotten to know Leslie pretty well," Mr. Linwood noted, laughing.

"I'm Jessica Wakefield, and this is Anna Barrett," Jessica said. She was very excited to be around such important people. All this glamour suited her just fine. She wished that the party could go on forever.

"Why don't we go in here where we can talk?" Mr. Linwood suggested, motioning to a cozy room with a fireplace. Jessica, Leslie and Anna followed the Linwoods into the room. They each sat down in comfortable, soft chairs that were arranged around a fireplace.

"Jessica, how did you recognize the spy?" Mr. Linwood asked.

Jessica grinned, pleased to be asked. "I recognized him by his ring. He was wearing a big diamond ring. It looked very expensive. I noticed it when we were upstairs, hiding in the study."

"You are very observant, young lady," Mr. Linwood remarked, obviously impressed. "If it hadn't been for your identifying him, he might have escaped!"

Jessica felt extremely important and proud of herself. But she said very modestly, "I'm glad I was able to help."

"What brings you to our party?" Mrs. Linwood asked. "Do your families work at the embassy?"

Anna and Jessica looked at each other.

"Not exactly, er, no," Jessica admitted.

"It's kind of a long explanation," Anna offered, glancing at Leslie. "You see, we're in Washington because we're contestants in the National Middle School Choral Competition. Our school is Sweet Valley Middle School, in Sweet Valley, California," Anna told them.

"That doesn't really explain why you're in the Australian Embassy," Mrs. Linwood said, looking amused.

Anna went on. "About three weeks ago, I found out in a letter to my parents that you were coming to Washington—and that I was Leslie's sister!" Anna laughed and winked at Leslie. "Well, I thought then that I had a long-lost sister."

Mr. and Mrs. Linwood glanced at each other. Jessica tried to figure out what they must be thinking. In all these years, they had never told Leslie he had a sister, just as Anna's parents had kept the truth from her.

"I tried out for the choral group just so I could get to Washington," explained Anna. "You see, I'm not much of a singer, but I had to come. I had to come to the embassy to find Leslie," she said softly.

"That is quite a story, Anna," Mrs. Linwood said, shaking her head in amazement.

Just then, there was a commotion coming from the other room. Anna stopped talking, and Mr. Linwood opened the door to see what was going on.

"We know they're in here somewhere!" Jessica heard a familiar voice explain impatiently.

"We must find our girls," said another familiar voice.

Jessica turned to Anna. "Oh, no—guess who's here."

Sure enough, a few seconds later, Mr. Stefan and Mrs. Isaacs appeared in the doorway of the small room.

"There you are!" Mrs. Isaacs shouted. "We've been looking everywhere for you!"

Jessica felt like sinking through the floor. Up

until now, no one had really noticed them. She felt as though she fit in at the embassy. But now she could hear the guests starting to talk about the unexpected arrivals.

"It has to do with someone's children," she heard someone say.

This wasn't the kind of attention Jessica wanted. Some photographers crowded in the open doorway. Jessica looked the other way so they couldn't take her picture.

"What are you doing here?" cried Mrs. Isaacs. "We've been worried out of our minds!"

"Why did you do this?" Mr. Stefan chimed in. "We were counting on you girls."

Anna took a deep breath. "Mr. Stefan, some things are more important to me than music."

Mr. Stefan put his hand to his forehead. Jessica and Anna looked at each other. Then Anna told Mr. Stefan the whole story.

"You mean you got into the choral group and you can't sing?" Mrs. Isaacs practically screeched. Her face had turned beet red.

"Yes. That's right," Anna replied sheepishly.

"I can't believe it!" huffed Mrs. Isaacs. She turned to Jessica. "And what are you doing here, young lady? Don't tell me you can't sing, either!"

"She's got a great voice. She just agreed to help me get to the embassy because she knew how important it was to me," Anna said on behalf of her friend.

"That's right," Jessica said.

"Excuse me. I'm Ambassador Linwood," Mr. Linwood greeted the two. "And this is my wife, Amy, and my son, Leslie."

"Ambassador Linwood!" they both said at once, looking at each other in embarrassment and shaking hands with the Linwood family.

"Excuse us for barging in like this," Mr. Stefan said apologetically. "But we've been so worried about these girls—out in the Washington streets alone. We had no idea where they could have gone."

"You can't imagine," grumbled Mrs. Isaacs, shaking her head. "I'm just so grateful that they're safe."

"Look, I don't know what rules they broke and I'm not making any excuses," Ambassador Linwood said. "But your girls here are very brave. You see, a spy broke into the embassy earlier tonight. Jessica, Anna and Leslie, my son, saw him steal some important documents and alerted me immediately. The spy is now in the hands of the proper authorities. If it wasn't for these three youngsters, the man might've gotten away with top secret information, which could have threatened our national security," he went on. "We must congratulate them on their bravery and quick thinking."

"Really?" Mrs. Isaacs looked completely dumbfounded. "Our girls?"

"Yes, your girls." Mr. Linwood smiled. "I wouldn't be too hard on them, if I were you."

"Can you imagine that? Jessica and Anna!" Mr. Stefan said. "I never would've guessed that some of my students would get involved in something like this. I thought we only came here to sing!"

Mr. Stefan and Mrs. Isaacs looked at the two girls as though they were seeing them for the first time. Jessica smiled smugly. She was very excited by what the ambassador said. After all, he *was* the ambassador! Imagine that! Anna was sort-of related to a famous person!

"It kind of happened by accident," Anna admitted quietly.

Jessica jabbed her with her elbow. "What do you mean?" she whispered. "We saw him take the papers, and we identified him later. It was no accident."

"I guess you're right," Anna said.

"I can't wait to see Sherrie Dunston's face when she hears about this," Jessica went on gleefully. "She'll never believe that we were involved in capturing an international spy. We're heroines!" Jessica couldn't wait to tell her classmates about her heroism. She knew that everyone in the choral group would be very impressed.

"I don't know what we would have done without them," Jessica heard Mrs. Linwood say. "We could never have identified the spy ourselves. He was dressed in a chef's outfit, and with his disguise he looked exactly like our real chef!"

"Oh, how frightening!" cried Mrs. Isaacs. "You must have been terrified!"

"And to think the girls were brave enough to find him," offered Mr. Stefan. "We'll have to celebrate when we get back to the hotel."

"Why not start now?" Mr. Linwood suggested.

"Let me just call the hotel," said Mrs. Isaacs. "I know everyone will be relieved."

A waiter came in a moment later and served everyone drinks. The girls and Leslie stood together.

One of the photographers came over to Mr. Linwood. "Could we have a few pictures of the girls and your son, Mr. Linwood?"

"Oh, certainly," Mr. Linwood said. "If it's OK with them."

Of course, Jessica was eager. Anna and Leslie stood with their arms around each other and smiled into the cameras.

"Just think," whispered Jessica. "We'll be in tomorrow's papers. Sherrie Dunston's going to turn green with envy!"

"Here's to the Sweet Valley Middle School Choral Group!"

Mr. Stefan approached Anna. "Now I understand why you were never around during rehearsals. Well, under the circumstances, I will excuse you from the group. You won't have to sing, Anna."

"Oh, thank you, Mr. Stefan," she said. "I'm sorry that I joined the group for the wrong reasons, but I wanted to come to Washington so badly."

"I understand," Mr. Stefan said. He turned to Mr. and Mrs. Linwood. "Will you be our guests at the competition on Monday?"

"We would love to come, Mr. Stefan," Mr. Linwood said, looking fondly at Anna. "We wouldn't want to miss it for the world!"

Fourteen

◇

The next morning, Elizabeth was awakened by the telephone ringing. Groggily, she picked up the receiver.

"Hello?" she asked.

"Hello. Anna?" a voice asked.

The events of the night before came back to Elizabeth in a blur. Anna had found her sister, who turned out to be her brother. And Jessica and Anna were heroines . . .

"Just a minute, I'll go get her," Elizabeth said. "May I ask who's calling?"

"Her mother."

She tumbled out of bed to get Anna. Anna was still asleep in the adjoining room, but Elizabeth shook her to wake her up. She figured it must be important.

"Anna, your mother is on the phone," Elizabeth said urgently. "You'd better talk to her."

Anna blinked sleepily and crawled out of bed to the phone. Elizabeth sat on her bed, listening to Anna's end of the conversation.

"You're here! Right now?" Anna squeaked in surprise. "You're coming right up?"

Anna hung up and turned to Elizabeth. "My parents are here! They just flew in. The ambassador phoned them last night and told them the whole story. My parents were worried and thought that they should be here with me. They want to meet the ambassador, too, and then tell Leslie and me together what happened." Anna brushed her hair out of her face. "Isn't this exciting?"

"It sure is." Elizabeth had to agree.

"I'm so tired from everything," Anna confided, sighing happily. "Last night I was chased by a spy and found my long-lost brother, and today my parents are here. And now I'm going to learn the whole truth about my family." She turned to Elizabeth with happy tears in her eyes. "Everything is happening so fast!"

Elizabeth wrapped an arm around her friend. "I think it's wonderful that your parents flew all the way here to be with you. I know you'll feel better having them around. And remember, you wanted to find out the whole truth. That's why you came here."

Anna smiled. "Thanks, Elizabeth. You're right. I did want to know the whole truth."

A few seconds later, there was a knock on the door. Elizabeth tiptoed across the room to answer it. Mr. and Mrs. Barrett stood on the threshold, and Anna flew into their waiting arms.

"I'm so glad you're here!" she cried, feeling relief and happiness flood over her. "It's okay, honey," her father said soothingly. "Everything is all right now."

"Jessica, you were wonderful!" Elizabeth exclaimed after Jessica had sung her solo beautifully at the dress rehearsal on Sunday.

"I'm really glad," Jessica said, beaming. "Between being an international spycatcher and a star soprano, I've got a lot of responsibility."

"Oh, please!" moaned Ellen. "Give us a break!"

The girls giggled. The dress rehearsal had gone well all around. The Sweet Valley chorus was dressed in black robes, with red trim. The girls wore red ribbons in their hair. The Grant School kids wore gold and blue robes, and the girls also wore matching ribbons.

"I think we should have purple robes instead of black," said Jessica, as they walked out of the auditorium.

"This isn't a Unicorn choir," Elizabeth reminded her. She was relieved that only two of the

Unicorns were in the choral group. They usually liked to run the whole show.

"I'm really glad Mr. Stefan didn't take you out of the group, Jessica. I was afraid he might be angry and do that," Anna said.

"Me, too. I mean, I really like catching spies at embassies, but I wouldn't want to miss out on the biggest moment of my singing career."

Elizabeth shook her head. "It looks like we're never going to hear the end of this."

Just then, Elizabeth saw the *Washington Eagle* on a newsstand. At the bottom of the page there was a picture of Anna and Jessica and Leslie! Underneath, the caption read: CHILDREN SOLVE CRIME AT AUSSIE EMBASSY.

"Look, Jess, Anna, Ellen!" Elizabeth cried, scooping up the paper. There wasn't any information on the spy, only the mention of Jessica, Anna, and Leslie being proclaimed heroes by the Linwoods.

"Oh, I can't believe it! It's so exciting!" cried Jessica.

"I think we should make a sign saying, " 'Jessica Wakefield—International Spycatcher and Heroine.' That way, everyone will know," suggested Anna.

"What a great idea!" Jessica agreed.

"That's my sister. Modest as always," teased Elizabeth.

The group took the bus back to the hotel and the girls went up to their rooms to change. Anna and her family and Jessica and Elizabeth had been invited to join the Linwoods for lunch at the embassy.

Jessica rummaged around in her suitcase for something special to wear.

"Jessica, hurry up. What's the big deal?" Elizabeth asked in exasperation. As usual, she was ready to go, dressed in a navy sweater and white corduroys while Jessica had on only her underwear.

"The embassy is a big deal, Elizabeth," explained Jessica. "It's not just an ordinary place. And," she fluttered her eyelashes like a movie star, "Leslie is going to be there."

"Oh. I knew there had to be a good reason," Elizabeth groaned. She had to admit, things had changed since Jessica had become interested in boys.

Jessica put on her new purple skirt and a lavender sweater. Then she found a sheer purple scarf and wrapped it around her blond hair. "How do I look?"

"You look like a gypsy," Elizabeth said, giggling. "Forget the scarf. Why don't you just put on a belt and we can go."

Jessica dug around in her suitcase for her belt. By the time she found it, half of her clothes lay on the floor.

When she was finally ready, the girls hurried out the door to join the others. Anna, her family and the twins took a cab over to the embassy.

* * *

The Linwoods greeted their guests in a different dining hall than the one that Jessica and Anna had been in the night before. Jessica wandered along behind the others, admiring the beautiful furnishings. This was a place fit for a queen, she decided. In a way, she sort of wished she were related to the ambassador so she could come here all the time.

"I thought we saw every room in this building," Anna said as they were led into the dining room.

"Almost," Mr. Linwood said. "We were thinking of hiring you two girls to give guided tours through the embassy."

Everyone laughed. Mrs. Linwood excused herself for a minute and returned with a two-year-old girl with blond hair and round blue eyes. "And this is our daughter, Jennifer," she said, holding the little girl so everyone could say hello to her.

Everyone sat down at the long antique table, with Mr. and Mrs. Linwood at either end. Jessica made sure she got a seat next to Leslie. Anna sat between Elizabeth and her mother.

"Well, it seems that Anna has had a lot of excitement since she arrived in Washington," Mrs. Barrett remarked. "She even got her picture in the paper!"

Mrs. Linwood looked at Anna and smiled. "Yes, Anna is the reason that we're all here today," she said. "If she hadn't found out about Leslie, we probably never would have met in person."

"Why not?" asked Anna.

"We believed we were doing the right thing for you children by keeping you from knowing about each other," explained Mr. Linwood. "Because of my government job at the time of your adoption, it was necessary that I keep a low profile."

"Mark wasn't even allowed to tell me anything about his work during that time," Mrs. Linwood added.

"I took a top-secret government post just before the adoption. It seemed like a good opportunity at the time, but I never realized it would lead to living so secretively."

"That sounds awful!" Elizabeth cried sympathetically.

"In many ways, it was," Mrs. Linwood continued. "I stayed home with Leslie because I was afraid to leave him alone very much. My husband and I decided that to protect the Barretts we'd ask them not to tell Anna about her brother. Of course, we both told our children that they were adopted, but that's all."

"For years, we kept it a secret, but after I recently left that post and became the ambassador, there was no need to keep up the secrecy any longer. That's when I wrote to your parents, Anna, to let them know we were moving to Washington," Mr. Linwood explained.

"Why didn't you tell me then?" Anna asked her parents.

"Because we weren't sure what to say," Mrs. Barrett told her daughter. "You see, the secret had been kept for so long that we didn't know quite how to tell you about it. We figured we would discuss the matter with the Linwoods when they arrived in the United States."

"But you decided for us, Anna," Mr. Barrett said, smiling at Anna. "When we learned you were coming to Washington with the choral group, we really had no idea that you planned on trying to find Leslie. We didn't know that you knew about him."

"I found the letter Mr. Linwood wrote to you," Anna confessed. "And I had to find a way to meet him. I was really disappointed when you didn't say anything about Leslie before I came to Washington."

"We're really sorry, honey. Please try to understand what happened," Mrs. Barrett said, putting an arm around Anna.

"I think I do," Anna replied. "It's just hard to imagine that all those years I had a brother I didn't even know about."

"Well, now you can get to know me!" Leslie said, laughing. "Here I am—and you've got a few more days in Washington, right?"

Anna giggled. "Right. We'll have to make up for the last twelve years!"

The Linwoods and the Barretts smiled at one another.

"I think we made a mistake keeping you a secret from each other," Mr. Linwood said. "And I'm really sorry for that. But I'm glad we're all together now."

The same evening, back at the hotel, there was a social hour with all the other contestants in the Choral Competition. Jessica was dressed in one of Elizabeth's party dresses since the only one she had brought had turkey stains on it.

"Uh, oh, look who's coming," Ellen said, nudging Jessica in the arm. "If it isn't the star of the Grant School Chorus," Jessica said sarcastically as Sherrie Dunston approached.

Sherrie was wearing a pink dress dotted with blue flowers. "Hi, Jessica. Hi, Anna," she oozed. "Is it really true you caught a spy last night?"

"What if we did?" Anna replied coolly. "What do you care?"

"What was the embassy like," Sherrie went on, unfazed.

"Were there any cute boys there? Or anyone famous?"

"Oh, there were tons of famous people," replied Jessica, twirling dreamily on her tiptoes. "It was so fabulous, so elegant—you would've *died*!"

"You're such a liar, Jessica Wakefield," Sherrie

replied angrily. "I'll bet you just made the whole story up so you wouldn't get in trouble."

"She is not a liar," Anna said on Jessica's behalf. "I was there, and I know. There is one especially cute boy there—and he's going to come to the competition tomorrow night!"

"Sure there is," cried Sherrie. She smiled smugly and stalked off.

Jessica and Anna doubled over laughing, and Ellen joined in. Suddenly, Jessica noticed Elizabeth looking at her in annoyance. "Oh, Lizzie, what's the matter?" she asked, going over to her twin.

"I'm surprised at you, Jess," Elizabeth said. "Now everyone from Grant School is going to be talking about how you and Anna were off boy chasing and just made up the spy part to cover yourselves."

"So what?" Jessica cried, throwing her hands into the air. "Sherrie made up that story about the boys to get back at you," Elizabeth tried to explain.

"That's the whole idea, don't you see, Lizzie?" Jessica said. "She made up that lie to get me in trouble so I'd get kicked out of the competition. But it didn't work. If I just ignore her silly lie now, it really makes her plan backfire."

A crystal-clear soprano voice rose from the next room, and a hush fell over the gathering. Everyone, including Jessica, Anna and Elizabeth, moved toward the sound.

Sherrie Dunston stood by the fireplace, her hand resting on the grand piano, singing a solo. She looked like an angel, with the firelight dancing in her hair and over her pretty face.

Elizabeth sighed, watching Sherrie. The girl had everyone's attention. "She might not be a very nice person," Elizabeth said. "But she sure can sing."

Fifteen

◇

"Did you see Leslie?" Jessica asked Anna and Elizabeth, peering around the backstage curtain to look at the audience.

It was Monday night, and the auditorium was full. Jessica pointed out the Linwoods, who were sitting next to Anna's parents. "Doesn't he look handsome?" she exclaimed. For the occasion, Leslie was wearing a dark suit and tie.

"They all look pretty handsome," Anna replied proudly.

"You're right, Anna," said Elizabeth. "Why don't you go down and sit with them so you can be together?"

"I will. I just wanted to thank you guys for helping me," Anna said. "You know, I wouldn't even be in Washington if it wasn't for you. Thank you for helping me stay in the group long enough to meet Leslie."

"Long enough for *me* to meet Leslie, too," Jessica said. "I'm glad it all turned out okay for you."

"Me, too," said Anna, laughing. "Good luck. I'll be cheering for you."

"Thanks," the twins said in unison.

Anna hurried out to the audience to be with her family. She looked at Leslie and his parents, and her own parents sitting next to them. She had always wanted to be a part of a big family, and now, in a way, she was.

Everything has turned out better for me than I had ever dreamed, she thought to herself. *I couldn't wish for a better brother than Leslie.*

Then the conductor came out to introduce the contestants, followed by Mr. Stefan.

"I am the director of the Sweet Valley Middle School Choral Group, from Sweet Valley, California. Our soloists tonight include Dana Larson and Jessica and Elizabeth Wakefield."

The audience applauded as Dana and the twins walked out and took their bows.

"Dana will sing an old English ballad," said Mr. Stefan, "followed by the Wakefield twins who will be singing some baroque Christmas pieces. Then we will join the rest of the choir." He motioned to the girls to take their places on stage.

After Dana finished her solo, Elizabeth gave Jessica's hand an affectionate squeeze and motioned for her to go first. Jessica smiled at the audience and clasped her hands in front of her. She took a deep breath, and then her voice soared through the auditorium, clear and strong. When she was finished, the applause rose from the audience.

"That was great, Jess," breathed Elizabeth, giving her sister a quick kiss on the cheek.

"Now it's your turn, Elizabeth," Ms. McDonald said.

Elizabeth stepped to the center of the stage. There was a hush, an expectant pause and then she began.

Her voice echoed beautifully in the big auditorium. When she was finished, the crowd went wild with enthusiastic applause. Elizabeth bowed and walked off the stage.

She found Jessica in the dressing room, touching up her lip gloss and brushing her hair.

"Come on, Jess. It's almost time for the whole choir to sing!"

"OK. I'm ready," Jessica replied. "I can't wait to beat Sherrie Dunston in the Dueling Voices competition."

Elizabeth nodded as she led the way back to the stage.

Elizabeth took her place in the back riser of the group in between Ellen and Bruce Patman. Sweet Valley's performance was dazzling. The crowd applauded loudly when they were done.

The judges scribbled notes furiously. Everyone's spirits soared.

Next were Conway Middle School, Johnson Middle School and Freeburg School. All of them gave great performances, but still, the Sweet Valley gang thought they were the best.

Finally came Grant Middle School. The Sweet Valley contestants listened nervously to the group's expert presentation. Sherrie and a couple of other students had solos during the songs.

"That's what I call competition," Bruce Patman said. "Listen to that horrible girl sing! She sure is good."

Elizabeth said, "Oh, come on, Bruce. She's not as good as we are."

"We'll see how good she is," Jessica grumbled.

Finally, Grant was finished. The crowd clapped enthusiastically. Then it was time for "Dueling Voices," a solo competition that was open to any singer from any school. From Sweet Valley, Dana, Jessica, Ellen and Winston Egbert had entered.

Students from rival schools were to sing alternating passages of the same song. Dana gave a dazzling performance against a student from the Freeburg School. Jessica was pitted against Sherrie in the second song.

Everyone who knew that the two girls were enemies cheered loudly.

"This is almost as good as a wrestling match," said Bruce, rubbing his hands together.

Jessica began the song. She sang until the conductor cut her off and directed Sherrie to begin. Sherrie's voice soared loud and clear, trembling on the last note. Jessica sang the next piece lightly, her voice dancing over the notes. When it was all over, Sherrie scowled at her. The crowd applauded.

"More! More!" the audience yelled. The conductor told Jessica and Sherrie to do one more song.

The girls' voices blended very well although Sherrie's voice trembled a little now and then.

When Jessica was finished, the Sweet Valley singers congratulated her. "You know, Sherrie's a good singer, but she's not half as good as you," Winston said, grinning.

"Really? Oh, Winston, you're great," Jessica said, eyes shining with excitement. "I just hope we win."

The judges sat busily tallying their scores while the students waited with nervous anticipation. After what seemed like an eternity, the conductor came out to announce the winners. "We've had a tough decision to make this evening," he began. "We have some of the finest young singers from across America here with us tonight. First, I give the award for the Best *New* Middle School Choral Group in America. That prize goes to Johnson Middle School of Madison, Wisconsin."

A whoop rose from one section of the audience, and everyone applauded. The whole Johnson group came up to receive their trophy and a ribbon for each contestant.

"For the past three years," continued the conductor, "Grant Middle School has taken first prize in the Best American Middle School Choral Group in this competition. They are a top notch group, let me tell you. But this year, the competition has been even tougher. I'm sad, but at the same time, happy, to announce that second place this year goes to Grant Middle School."

Sherrie Dunston clapped her hands to her face in shock. She glanced over at the Sweet Valley kids in horror.

"Serves her right," whispered Jessica. "I'm so glad they didn't win."

Sherrie didn't get up to receive the group's prize. Instead, she just sat there trying to overcome the shock of not having won.

"It must be hard to lose the title after so many years," Elizabeth said sympathetically.

"We have a new winner this year—the group from Sweet Valley, California. Doesn't that sound like a nice place to live?" the conductor joked. The audience laughed. Some Grant School kids booed. "May I congratulate our new winners—the Sweet Valley Middle School Choral Group!"

The Sweet Valley section streamed onto the stage, hugging and kissing each other wildly. No one could stand still long enough to receive the trophy. Seeing this, Elizabeth strode up to the podium and accepted the trophy on behalf of her group.

"Thank you everyone for this wonderful prize. We are pleased to be here and to be a part of this great competition," she said, holding up the gold trophy for everyone to see.

The crowd went wild. Finally, the Sweet Valley kids left the stage.

"And now for our individual singers. First prize in the Soprano Soloist competition goes to Elizabeth Wakefield of Sweet Valley. In the alto competition, first place goes to Dana Larson, also from Sweet Valley, who sings both soprano and alto parts. For the "Dueling Voices" competition, we have Dana Larson from Sweet Valley for the alto competition. And for the first time ever, in the "Dueling Voices" soprano competition, there is a tie; the winners are: Jessica Wakefield and Sherrie Dunston. And in the boys' alto/counter-tenor "Dueling Voices" competition, Tyrone Seeley of Johnson Middle School takes first prize!"

The applause thundered through the large auditorium as the contestants went up to claim their prizes. Flashbulbs went off, people whistled and sang out.

"Sweet Valley is a bright and shining new star this year—taking away many of the prizes. But I want to thank all of the groups who participated here tonight," the conductor said in closing.

Jessica took her bows and rushed backstage to

meet with the others. She felt as if she were on top of the world. Imagine—tieing with Sherrie Dunston in the "Dueling Voices" competition!

"Congratulations!" cried Elizabeth, giving her a big hug. "I can't believe how well we all did! And Jessica, you were super!"

"Next year, I'm going to *beat* Sherrie," Jessica said with determination.

Anna walked over to Jessica with a bouquet of red roses wrapped in tissue paper.

"For me?" Jessica asked in amazement.

"Yes for you. Congratulations," said Anna. "They're not from me, but I want you and Elizabeth to know how happy I am for all of us."

"Thanks," Jessica and Elizabeth said at the same time.

"Well, read the card," urged Anna.

Jessica opened the small card and read the inscription: "Jessica—Congratulations to a great singer! See you at Carnegie Hall! Love, Leslie Linwood."

Jessica's eyes were shining as she showed the card to everyone standing nearby. Holding the roses, she really felt like the great singer Leslie said she was.

"Wow, I wish we weren't leaving Washington so soon. Are you ever lucky to have a brother like Leslie," Jessica told Anna as they hugged each other. Elizabeth joined in their embrace and they all agreed this was the most exciting thing that had ever happened.

SWEET VALLEY TWINS

We hope you enjoyed reading this book. If you would like to receive further information about titles available in the Bantam series, just write to the address below, with your name and address: Kim Prior, Bantam Books, 61–63 Uxbridge Road, Ealing, London W5 5SA.

If you live in Australia or New Zealand and would like more information about the series, please write to:

Sally Porter
Transworld Publishers
(Australia) Pty Ltd.
15-23 Helles Avenue
Moorebank
N.S.W. 2170
AUSTRALIA

Kiri Martin
Transworld Publishers (NZ) Ltd
Cnr. Moselle and Waipareira
Avenues
Henderson
Auckland
NEW ZEALAND

All Bantam Young Adult books are available at your bookshop or newsagent, or can be ordered from the following address: Corgi/Bantam Books, Cash Sales Department, PO Box 11, Falmouth, Cornwall, TR10 9EN.

Please list the title(s) you would like, and send together with a cheque or postal order. You should allow for the cost of the book(s) plus postage and packing charges as follows:

All orders up to a total of £5.00: 50p
All orders in excess of £5.00: Free

Please note that payment must be made in pounds sterling; other currencies are unacceptable.

(The above applies to readers in the UK and Republic of Ireland only)

B.F.P.O. customers, please allow for the cost of the book(s) plus the following for postage and packing: 60p for the first book, 25p for the second book and 15p per copy for the next 7 books, thereafter 9p per book.

Overseas customers, please allow £1.25 for postage and packing for the first book, 75p for the second book, and 28p for each subsequent title ordered.

Thank you!

The Phillip Schofield Fun File

Fed up with those Monday morning blues?

Living in mortal fear of tomorrow's maths exam?

Stuck in the house on a wet and windy Wednesday?

Let your favourite T.V. presenter cheer you up with his personal selection of jokes and puzzles, games and brain-teasers!

From wherever Bantam paperbacks are sold!

Grab your blanket, your pillow, your pyjamas and your toothbrush and get ready for some fun!

is coming soon from wherever Bantam paperbacks are sold.

Kate, Lauren, Stephanie, and Patti love having sleepover parties. Can anything beat having a few good friends round for the night, having midnight feasts, watching creepy movies, and playing Truth or Dare all night long?

The girls don't think anything can, and nor will you when you read this new series.